Rossen focused on the face of the driver, then dropped to the junction of the throat—that small hollow where doctors insert breathing tubes. He'd fire two rapid shots, letting the natural rise of the rifle place his second shot in the face of the driver. The pleasant, slightly sweet smell of thin gun oil tickled the hairs in his nostrils; it reminded him of some kind of candy he'd eaten long ago as a child.

The weapon was ready, the shooter was relaxed . . . his breathing became easy. Concentrate, always concentrate. He waited until the truck made a light curve that brought it face on to him. Then he let instinct take over . . . he didn't select the time to fire; his entire body did. Acting of its own accord, it knew when it was right and he had learned long ago to listen to it . . .

RUN
FOR THE
SUN

BARRY SADLER

RUN
FOR THE
SUN

TOR

A TOM DOHERTY ASSOCIATES BOOK

RUN FOR THE SUN

Copyright © 1986 by Barry Sadler

All rights reserved, including the right to reproduce this book or portions thereof in any form.

First printing: January 1986

A TOR Book

Published by Tom Doherty Associates
49 West 24 Street
New York, N.Y. 10010

ISBN: 0-812-58829-0
CAN. ED.: 0-812-58830-4

Printed in the United States of America

0 9 8 7 6 5 4 3 2 1

Prologue

Among some tribes of the Maya there is the legend of a mighty warrior, a warrior who slew his enemies upon the field of battle and counted victories without number. But he was a man of great pride, without love or compassion, and for his sin of pride his soul was taken from him by the sun god. He was doomed to wander the earth until eternity faded unless he could reclaim his soul.

For long years he made sacrifice on the altars of the god Kulkulcan, and at last he had a vision. He was given the gift of strength by the god, and with it he was to chase the sun until he reclaimed his soul, that he might rest.

From that ancient time to now, in the highlands of the Maya it is said around the fires that if you look very carefully into the evening disk of the sun god, you can see El Perdido, the Lost One,

Running, running for the sun. . . .

1

Searing flames reached out. Jellied gasoline turned the interior of the machine-gun bunker into an inferno. A man ran screaming from the entrance, his entire body wrapped in flames, eyes melting in their sockets, to fall facefirst, his legs and arms drawing up under him as the fires shriveled the tendons and muscles, shrinking them. Inside the bunker were more screams that silenced abruptly as ammunition began to explode, mercifully tearing those inside to shreds. He tried to move but couldn't. He was hung in the barbed wire, his right leg twisted under him, bone splinters protruding through the fabric of his camouflage trousers. The flames began to move down the trench closer to him. He tried to squirm out of the concertina, but entangled himself only more, the prongs of the wire eating into his flesh, but he didn't feel them. He felt only the flames washing the side of the trench. Blood poured from a hundred cuts, where he'd torn deep wounds in the course of his strug-

2

gles. The flames came closer and he heard voices. Chinese.

Raising his eyes, he saw the Chinese with the Russian-made flamethrower. He had stopped hosing the trench and was looking for new targets. His eyes touched those of the man trapped in the wire. Brown eyes set in their epicanthic folds smiled at his victim as he swung the nozzle of the flamethrower over. Finger on the igniter, the Chinese began to take in the slack that would let loose a touch of hell on the trapped American.

Eyes jerked open to the ringing of the phone. His back stuck to the thin sheets. The cold sweat covering him had the stink of fear to it. A sour acid odor that came all too often in the night. The phone rang again. He checked the time. Two in the morning. Before the third ring ended, he lifted the receiver, setting the earpiece to the side of his head as he lay back down, shifting his body to get away from the unpleasant dampness his pores had released.

"Hello. . . ."

The operator in the lobby asked in tinny tones, "Señor Rossen?" Wiping the night sweat from his eyes with the back of his hand, he grumbled, "Yeah, I mean *sí*. Rossen *aqui*."

"*Momentito, por favor.*"

Rossen waited, wondering who was calling him at that hour. His answer came as the overseas line crackled, then cleared. The voice on the other end was thin and distant. "Rossen, Phü Nhãm. Is that you?"

Rossen gave an involuntary groan. The only one who ever called him Phü Nhãm, killer, was Tomanaga, his former backup man from the days when they'd worked together as a sniper team in 'Nam. Tommy was short, tough, and steady. They had worked together on different jobs several times after they'd separated (*nice word, sounds like a divorce in process*) from the army.

"Yeah, Tommy, it's me. What the hell are you doing calling me at this hour, and how did you find me?"

"I am sorry to wake you, my friend, but I had to make certain you would be there when I arrive tomorrow. We have work to do."

Rossen straightened up, setting his feet on the now gray, once red throw rug beside his bed.

"What can you tell me about the contractor?" There was a pause on the far end of the line before Tommy came back. He selected his words carefully, though it was extremely unlikely that there would have been an unwelcome listener anywhere on the line. "We are going into business with some Latin gentlemen. Read the London *Times* of the fourteenth, international section, third article." Rossen grunted an agreement.

"Xa Phai."

"I will arrive in Guatemala City on flight two four seven at nine P.M. your time. Meet me at the gate after I clear customs."

Rossen ran a hand through his short-cropped sandy hair, its peppered flecks of gray growing in number daily lately.

"I'll be there."

He knew, without having to see him, that Tommy was smiling on the other end of the line. Tommy always smiled when he got Rossen into deep shit.

"Rossen?" Tommy's voice changed. "Did you know that Colonel Hatch died yesterday in L.A.? Heart attack."

Rossen groaned. "Oh, shit. . . ." He'd been waiting for Hatch to contact him about a job. He and Tommy had often worked for the old mercenary leader on hostage recoveries in South America and other places. Now the old man was dead. Another dinosaur sucked up in the world's tar pit. There weren't many like him left alive. Former OSS under Donovan in World War II, one-time advisor in the late forties to a war lord in northern China. Hatch was one of the best, and the last of his breed.

"Did you hear me, Rossen?"

"Yes, I heard you. What else is there to say? The old man is gone, that's all there is to it. When did you say you were coming in?"

Tommy's voice switched back into its familiar style. "*Shimpai nai, Phü Nhäm*. I will see you tomorrow night at twenty-one hundred hours. 'Til then, *Kyo skite*."

"Yeah, I'll take it easy. Good-bye." Rossen replaced the receiver, idly wondering how many of the ugly black phones Ma Bell had sold Central America before they discovered phones came in different colors.

He got up. The floor was gritty under his feet. He didn't *want* to go back to work, but man lived not by whiskey alone. He was awake now, his mind turning over what Tommy had said. The Latino business, and that he was coming to Guatemala. Rossen didn't wonder or care much just what the job was. He needed to do something to clear the shit from his brain. Besides, Tommy wouldn't work for just anyone. They had to be the good guys, or at least as close as they could get to being the good guys. Down here it was sometimes hard to even tell who the hell the players were, forget the good guys. Tommy had a knack for locating people who needed their kind of expertise. What was the date on the London *Times*? The fourteenth, yesterday. There'd probably be one at the British embassy.

Restless, the nightmare still with him, he moved across the hotel room to the window, pulling the cord to raise the venetian blinds, which were the color of very old ivory. Outside was third *avenida, zona uno*. Not exactly the best part of town. Leaning his face against the grime-streaked window, he looked down. The streets still moved with the shadows of a few night people on whatever quest they had set for themselves. Some were hunters; others the prey. He knew the feelings of both. Disgusted with himself, he let the blinds back down and went into the bathroom. Turning on the faucet, he resisted the temptation to drink out of it. In these places you never knew what would be on them, though he sometimes doubted that a decent bacteria could even live in his body. Cupping his hands under the faucet, he rinsed his face, then rubbed the back of his neck as he examined his reflection between the flyspecks on the sink's mirror.

The face looking back at him was tired. Not just tired from lack of sleep, tired from too much living and too much death. Once it had been a face that even mothers trusted their daughters with—clean-looking· and clear-eyed. Now it looked like a tank had used it as a parking spot. The nose—twisted over to the right, a bit off center. Deep-set eyes made his face look thinner than it actually was. His arms and body still showed signs of abnormal strength in the thin, narrow bands of muscle. And the scars, including several of the peculiar roundish pucker marks that showed where bullets had entered his hide on more than one occasion. The last one was only four months old, a souvenir of the Arab Emirates. The hairline was beginning to lose its war, too. Every year it was retreating a bit farther from his forehead. He wondered if the gray was going to beat the skin, and decided that probably the skin would win. He was forty-five, and tonight he looked closer to fifty than to forty.

Tommy had perfect timing. He had just finished a two-week bout beginning with a bottle of Jack Daniel's that his good buddy and bar owner Freddie Gernandt had rounded up for him someplace, and ending up with whatever had alcohol in it. Stepping back to get a better look at the picture before him, he sucked in a breath of air and let it out, then took a pinch of the loose skin around his waist between his fingers. *Shit*, he thought sullenly. *I hope that we don't have to walk to wherever it is Tommy has us set for. Vive la mort, vive la guerre, vive le sacré mercenaire!*

He took a towel from the single rack, wet it, and took a whore's bath, rinsing off the night sweat his dreams had brought to him. The dreams came too often; he wondered if he needed to see a shrink. A shiver rolled over him. The night was warmer than usual. Normally, Guatemala City had pleasant temperatures, in the sixties and seventies, all year round, but tonight it was stifling. Must be the rains coming in from the gulf side.

Flamethrowers were his bogeyman. He hated the damned things. The memory of cooking human bod-

ies screaming and writhing as the liquid fire ate them
made his stomach churn. With difficulty he resisted
the temptation to open the dresser and take a pull at
the half pint of rum made by the Castillo family. This
was not the time to drink, not if he was going back to
work again.

Suddenly, the confines of the dingy room became
too close. He needed to breathe. He was awake now
and knew that he wouldn't be able to get back to
sleep. He dressed in faded jeans and a short-sleeve
blue shirt, over which he put a lightweight khaki
bush jacket. He went to the dresser and opened the
top drawer. Leaving the double action .380 Mauser
and the rum alone, he took out his watch and put it
on, thinking that Tommy had called just in time. He
was down to his last ten quetzales and the Rolex
would have been going to Freddie at the Club Europa
in the morning. As an afterthought he pushed a pair
of white cotton socks over and took out a knife with
a wooden grip. He gave it a habitual flick of his
wrist, throwing the blade straight out of the handle,
pushed down the lock catch with his thumb, reversed
the process, and put the gravity knife into his jacket
pocket. The weight of the old World War II German
paratrooper's weapon felt solid and comfortable.

He left his room and went down the two flights of
stairs to the lobby. The night clerk of the Centrale
looked up from his paper and nodded at the gringo,
not really caring; it was just a habit to see who was
coming and going. Once, the hotel had catered to
better and wealthier clientele, but like the street outside, it had given way to time and decay.

A bored security guard in what looked like a cast-
off marine dress uniform unlocked the door for him,

noting that as the "Pendeho," Rossen, the "chapin," went out into the streets, he didn't seem to care whether the rent-a-cop thought he was dumb or not.

The first feel of the night air was heavy, oppressive. Heat soaked up in the sidewalks during the day radiated upward to ride the thin currents of polluted air that moved between the buildings. Lights from windows and streetlamps were hazed by a thin veil of mist that had ridden in from the mountains surrounding the city. Normally, he'd have been able to see at least one of the huge volcanoes on the horizon, but there was no moon this night.

Traffic was thin in this section of town, and no one stopped if they didn't have to. The few who did were checking out the street whores, not all of them women. Young boys in tight jeans stood on corners or in doorways of shuttered tiendas. Rossen went on up to Fifth Avenida and Calle 1, passing small knots of transvestites with overlarge hands and feet and mock New York makeup and hairstyles. They didn't call out to him, knowing that he was not a customer. They'd seen him several times over the last few weeks and with accurate instincts knew he was one to leave alone.

Rossen nodded at them absently; several of the boy-girls looked a lot better than the regular working girls on the streets. They certainly did their hair and clothes better. Three blocks away was an all-night café that catered to night people and the lost who had nowhere else to go and for the price of a cup of coffee were permitted to spend an hour inside away from the danger of the streets. Another cup of coffee, and they were granted another hour's grace. Otherwise—out and make a place for the next one.

Rossen was the only Anglo on the street that night. To anyone watching, he was just another unshaven, middle-aged, tired-looking man who had a Rolex on his wrist.

Jesus Lopez and Carlos Cordon had the sharp eyes of youth. Youthful predators. Both spotted the expensive watch at the same time as Rossen passed. They came to an agreement without speaking. They had a good idea of where their quarry was heading. Making a turn at the next corner, they ran around to the other side of the block, ignoring the trash cans and prone bodies of several Indians, who cursed at them for disturbing their sleep. They raced ahead onto the next block and cut back to where a vacant lot would face the approaching Rossen. They were waiting when he passed on his way to the coffee shop.

Rossen moved steadily down the street. Through habit, his hand stayed in his pocket, holding the comforting weight of the gravity knife. He did not expect any trouble. It was just a habit. His eyes missed nothing, not even the two slender young men in jeans and T-shirts who had passed. When they'd gone by, he'd waited a moment. They turned. They weren't in sight, and there was no place on that block they could have hidden in. They disappeared too fast. He fingered the release catch of the knife tentatively. Lights from two cars blanked his vision for a moment, and he moved his head away from the glare. At the next intersection a military-police car slowly pulled out, the camouflage-uniformed soldier in the driver's seat giving him a cursory once-over. Seeing nothing of interest—just a chapin out checking the whores—the soldier shoved the Galil assault rifle a little more to his right, where it wouldn't rub against his leg. The patrol car headed east; the *policia* didn't like this section of town any more than Rossen did.

One block ahead he could see the lights of the coffee shop and wished that he'd stayed in his room.

Jesus and Carlos waited in the vacant lot; the MPs in the patrol car hadn't even looked in their direction. Carlos risked a quick peek out from the lot, his breathing heavy from the unaccustomed exercise. The watch was coming to them. If it was one of the good Rolexes and not a counterfeit, they'd be able to get maybe a C-note for it. Both felt the pleasant warm anticipation of one about to make a kill. To let someone else feel their strength. It made them feel good, warm, and strong to see the fear in the eyes of those they chose to take. This gringo would be no different. Maybe they'd kill him, maybe not. If they did, he would be the first one.

Rossen felt a tingle in the small dark hair of his forearms and on the back of his hands, where tiny beads of sweat clung. His shirt was becoming damp and stuck to his back, and in his mouth he had begun to get the same acrid taste of the fear that had sweated out of his pores during his nightmare. Instinct or subconscious awareness, he knew that he wasn't going to make it to the coffee shop without something happening. Without being obvious, he began a sweep of the street in front of him, noting everything that could be seen: the streetlamps and lights from ash-covered windows, shadows where men could conceal themselves. His heart began to beat faster, the pulse in his throat gaining in strength as adrenaline began to pump through his system. He didn't change his

body attitude, nor did he quicken his pace to reach
the safety of the coffee shop; everything about him
was as before. He knew the most likely place for
anything to come down would be the empty lot twenty
feet in front of him. He moved closer to the gutter
side of the sidewalk so anyone there would have to
come out after him.

Jesus waited till Rossen reached the center of the
alley before showing himself. Stepping out quickly to
face the tired-looking man, he was full of confidence. There was nothing about this old son of a
bitch to show there was any fight in him. He'd be
easy meat. Carlos moved with him, standing a bit to
the side. Both had the apparently standard-issue stainless steel switchblade with black plastic handle in
their hands.

Rossen came to a stop, turning his body slightly to
the side. He said nothing, just glad that the weapons
in the two boys' hands were knives and not guns.

Jesus waved his knife to indicate that Rossen was
to get off the street and into the vacant lot, where
they wouldn't be disturbed.

"Andale, viejo!"

Rossen did as he was told though he objected to
being called an old man. He seemed to shrink as he
obeyed; a jerk on his right shoulder from Carlos
hurled him into the alley, his back up against the
wall. Just where he wanted to be. Jesus moved forward to take the watch, when Rossen's right hand
came out of his pocket, the weight of the Solingen
blade clicking the knife into place as his left swung
in a half circle, going over the top of Carlos's hand,
blocking the elbow and half-turning him to the outside. Rossen's knife laid open the punk's jugular,

slicing deep into the neck muscles until the white cartilage of the windpipe was exposed. Carlos's head hung half on, half off. There was a glazed, confused expression to the dying eyes, as if to say *This wasn't the way it's supposed to work!* His legs collapsed and blood gouted out of the wound, covering Jesus's chest with warm sticky fluid.

The Latino backed away. The man in front of him wasn't the same man they'd been trying to rob. The slouch and weary look were gone. Years had dropped away from the face. Jesus backed up until he was against the other side of the wall, a trash can blocking any movement to his left.

Rossen moved in slowly, his knife held low to his side along his leading right leg, the blade up, his left hand extended, fingers outstretched. Jesus waved his knife in front of him like a fan to keep this thing away from him. He knew death was close. Carlos's body lay draining in the dirt of the alley, legs trembling as if with St. Vitus's dance.

"Pero no, señor! Por amor de Dios, no!"

Rossen grunted. "It's a little late to ask me for the love of God. In a few seconds you can speak to him yourself." Jesus threw himself off the wall, his knife slicing the air in front of him. He was bigger and younger than the man in front of him; if he could get a grip on the *viejo*'s knife hand, then he'd have him.

Jesus lunged forward, the point of his knife going for Rossen's eyes. Reflexes built through long hard years brought Rossen's left hand up, his forearm blocking the thrust to his face . . . sliding along Jesus's forearm . . . turning to grab the boy's wrist . . . twisting it sideways . . . pushing the point of the switchblade away from his face. Jesus thought he'd made a good move, managing to get a grip on Rossen's knife hand, and tried to pull him off balance, only to feel the bones in his own wrist start to crack. *God-damn, the old s.o.b. was strong.* He tried to pull away; the bones gave a bit.

Rossen was content to let Jesus hang on to his knife hand for the moment. He didn't need it. Bones began to crack. Jesus's wrist snapped, the switch-blade falling to pavement. The pressure didn't quit; he was forced to his knees, tears running from his eyes as the pain of bones grinding against each other began to force a scream out of his throat. Rossen twisted his own wrist inside Jesus's grip, freeing his knife hand, and moved in. Dropping his body slightly, he swung his knee into the boy's face, crushing the cartilage in his nose, driving him back against the wall and stopping the would-be scream. Releasing his grip on Jesus's wrist, Rossen grabbed the thick mop of black hair and pulled him to his feet, slamming him against the wall of the building as his own knife came to rest just at McBurney's point. The place where doctors take out an appendix.

Jesus tried to speak, bloody foam coming from his crushed nose as he tried to breathe. He didn't feel very strong anymore. He was afraid, very afraid. His voice rose an octave as he looked up at the face above him.

"Señor Gringo. Está usted mi muerte?"

The tone of Jesus's words was more like that of a small child asking an awkward question of an adult. He had heard the same tones himself when he had been the one standing over a victim.

Rossen felt no compassion. There was no difference between this young face and those of enemy soldiers he had killed in a half-dozen wars. Speaking in Spanish for the first time, he said, "Yes. I am your death. . . ."

He raised the tip of his knife to where the thin skin of the chest covered the lower lobe of the heart, and pushed.

Jesus opened his mouth and whispered, *"Madre de Dios."* They were his last words.

Rossen let the body slide to lie silent in the dark of the empty trash-filled lot. He cleaned his knife on Jesus's shirt, pressed the lock catch to release the blade so it could slide back into its handle, and replaced it in his jacket pocket. Going to each body, he checked the pockets. Between them he came up with sixty-two quetzales and change. *Waste not, want not,* he thought. Hauling Jesus over to join Carlos, he covered them up with a couple of cardboard boxes and left them for the garbage men to find.

Stepping out of the lot, he checked left and right. The street was empty except for some late-night drinkers three blocks away. No one paid any attention to him, and if they'd known what had come down, no one would have said anything. It was none of their business. Several of the men and women asleep behind their windows or in the doorways of the buildings would have said a small prayer of thanks that at least two of those who preyed on them weren't going to be on the streets anymore.

Rossen had no regrets or pangs of conscience over the two young men he'd killed. As far as he was concerned, he'd just saved them and a lot of others a life of pain. He checked himself over by the glow of the streetlamp. There was blood on his hands and jacket. Taking his jacket off, he wiped his hands as clean as he could and folded the jacket so none of the bloodstains would show. He could wash up in the rest room of the coffee shop and get rid of the jacket in a trash can when he left. He felt a little better, but he really wanted a good hot cup of the rich dark Guatemalan coffee and maybe a roll. He was suddenly a bit hungry.

2

Traffic noise forced his eyes reluctantly open. After his late cup of coffee and doughnut, he'd returned to his room and fallen into a deep, dreamless sleep. Tumbling out of bed, he made it to the bathroom and groaned. It was typical for one of the lower class hostels. A toilet and shower with an electric flash heater on the spray nozzle. Cautiously, he reached in to turn on the hot water, hesitating before placing a finger on the handle. Closing his eyes, he twisted rapidly, then cursed as he got a jolt of electricity through his arm. That damned thing always bit him. The electric codes in Central America were almost nonexistent, and the flash heater did little more than raise the water to one or two degrees above body temperature . . . and that only when the weather was warm. Jumping in and out just fast enough to decontaminate, he dried with a thin cotton towel with an embroidered picture of a quetzal bird that looked as though it were ready to molt.

Leaving his key with the desk clerk, he went out into a day that was bright, crisp, and clear. The diesel fumes from the hundreds of overaged buses and trucks hadn't settled yet. The streets were crowded. He'd been surprised at first at the rapid pace of the people. He'd thought they'd be slow and easy-going. Instead, they moved like New Yorkers in a hurry.

Street vendors hawked their wares. Mangos, papayas, bananas, pineapples. Jeans and toothbrush stands all crowded together. Nearly everyone he saw was eating something. He asked Freddie about it once and was told it was some kind of national compulsion. The people of Guatemala were always eating.

At the corner near the Tejano restaurant, Rossen put a fifty-centavo bill in the hand of a wrinkled crone who sat in a doorway, a thin shawl covering her head and shoulders, her hand outstretched like the claw of a cadaver. Wrinkled fingers snapped shut when they felt paper money in them. The bill disappeared into her shawl, and the open hand begging alms was back in place in the space of a heartbeat. It had become a daily routine. When he got up in the morning he'd pass the old woman and put a fifty-centavo bill in her hand. Never once had she looked up to see who the donor was. Fifty centavos could keep her alive another day. Sometimes Rossen sat at Freddie's and watched the beggars on the streets and thought about the old ones. Was he doing them a kindness? Maybe it would be better to not give them anything and just let them go to sleep one night and not wake up the next morning. Was he just giving her enough to keep her suffering one more day? He pushed the thoughts away, as he always did. As long as the old woman had the strength to keep her hand open she wanted to live, and he'd keep putting the fifty-centavo notes into it. Life or death was her choice, not his.

He nodded briefly at two blue-uniformed, M1-carbine-carrying members of the Guardia. This was their area, and they'd been passing each other on a regular basis for a couple of weeks. They'd never spoken, but bit by bit the nervous looks of suspicion at this tall chapin had changed to one of acceptance. He knew they'd checked him out.

He crossed over in front of the Bank of America to the gray stone-faced building, owned by the Banco de Ejercito, the army's bank, where Freddie's Club Europa was open for business. Freddie turned and spotted him, smiled, and waved for him to come on up. He had already put on a pot of weak, watered-down coffee, knowing Rossen would be showing up as usual, within a half hour of his opening the doors. Freddie always made a weak pot for him. The strong native brew was usually too much for Rossen's tongue. He'd drink two cups of the local brew, then be on a caffeine high for three hours. Going up the stairs, Rossen nodded at one of the girls who worked at the travel agency two doors down from Freddie. Nice-looking lady. He smiled at the sign on Freddie's door, ENGLISH SPOKEN, then in small letters under it, BUT NOT UNDERSTOOD.

Freddie, already pouring the first cup, nodded as Rossen took his regular seat at the counter, where he'd have the best view of the street. Freddie had the best window in Guatemala. From it one could see every character-type the country had to offer. Mayan Indians from Chichicastenango or Huehuetenango. Smartly dressed secretaries and businessmen. Tough, sinewy campesinos, machetes at their sides, walking the streets of the big city for the first time. Colors and people, all kinds. It was a great window.

"*Qué tal, gringo?*" Freddie poured himself his morning shot of Johnnie Walker Red.

"Not much, Freddie. Just another day. What's for lunch today?"

Handing Rossen a menu that was never read, he puffed up his mustache and announced as he always did: "*Lomita con papas,* or, if you prefer, red cabbage and kielbasa."

"Naw, I think I'll stay with the *lomita*." Freddie was famous for his beef tenderloin. Somehow, sauerkraut in Guatemala just never seemed right, even if Freddie was German and so was a good portion of his clientele.

Freddie eyed Rossen's Rolex. "Ready to pay your bill yet?" Rossen knew he'd had his eye on the watch for a long time.

"Not yet, but I'll do it tomorrow. A friend's coming in tonight."

Cocking an eye at Rossen, Freddie received an okay and poured him a shot of scotch. Leaning over the bar, he touched Rossen's wrist with a forefinger. "Why don't you go home? You're my friend, but always I feel that trouble is just around the corner for you. And this part of the world is a good place to find it."

He knew that Freddie was speaking from concern. He also knew the German was right. Trouble was just around the corner.

"Where would I go, Freddie? And for what? Who knows, I might just decide to do like you and stay here, get married, and go into business." Freddie had jumped ship twenty-three years earlier with three dollars in his pocket. He loved the country, his Guatemalan wife, and his three kids. But he knew Rossen wasn't like him.

"Don't bullshit me, amigo. You draw too much attention, and if you stay here too long and keep doing the things you do, then someday someone is going to come after you. Go away and come back when things have settled down a bit. Right now everyone is touchy, especially about people in your line of work. Someone is going to kill you, and I don't want that to happen."

Rossen grinned at him. "And why not, you hard-nosed kraut?"

"Because you, *Schiesskopf,* if you get killed, I will never be able to collect the eighty quetzales you owe me. Why did you think, because you are so cute and good-humored?"

They changed the subject as more of Freddie's regulars came in. By lunchtime the small restaurant would be filled with teachers from the German school and Guatemalan businessmen or common workers. Freddie's was open to all, and all were welcome. Rich and poor mingled freely at the Club Europa.

Rossen sat watching through the window. At eleven-thirty the American school catty-corner from the restaurant let out for lunch. Teenaged boys and girls in dark blue and white passed by. Rossen could see why Freddie loved this country. If he'd had it in him, and wanted one place to settle down, this would have been his choice. The people were very old-world: gracious, good-hearted, and industrious. The climate was anything you wanted, from subtropical to the equivalent of Denver with palm trees.

Carlos Cordon came in, sat down beside him, and ordered the *lomita* and a Gallo beer. Like most of the others who had met Rossen, he thought the American was no more than a security specialist who had been out to several of the larger fincas and mines to advise on the best way to protect businesses from raids by the guerrillas. Half of them also thought he worked for the CIA. Part of what Freddie worried about was that one of the mines where Rossen had worked had been attacked in the last week, and the mine guards had eaten up the guerrillas' asses. If they found out that it was because of Rossen's efforts, they would come after him.

Rossen waited till after three, then paid his tab for the day with the money he'd picked up the night before—surprising Freddie a bit.

Heading back down to the street, he caught bus number fourteen, which would take him up to the Camino Real. It was closer to the airport.

Pushing his way through the crowded bus toward the rear door, he hung on to the backs of seats while the driver played demolition derby. Finally, an old Indian woman gathered up her baskets and pushed past him. He settled down, nodding at the curious looks of the student sitting next to him.

He liked the buses—for ten centavos you could ride all over the city. The bus turned up Avenida 7, hit the circle below the National Theatre, and headed down Embassy Row on the Avenida de la Reforma. Here the houses and buildings were more expensive than in the downtown area. French and Italian restaurants lined the broad thoroughfare. With nightfall the cafés would open up, and even though business for many of them was nearly nonexistent, they would be completely staffed with maître d's and waiters, chefs and hat-check girls, all waiting for the tourists who had gone away. Faithful and stubborn, they waited for them to return.

Through the open window he could smell the acrid odor coming from what he called pee trees along the sidewalks of the avenue. There was a lack of public facilities, so the locals who had stands on the Avenida—selling flowers and souvenirs to the few tourists and businessmen who still came to Guatemala—made use of the huge trees on the Reforma to ease their bladders.

At the Popol Vuh Museum he got off and walked across to the British embassy. Guatemalan security police asked to see his passport, and after comparing his picture with his now four-years-older and slightly more seedy face, they passed him through. Inside, he went to the information desk and asked if they still had a copy of the London *Times* for the fourteenth. He was inventoried with the look a maître d' reserves for winos seeking tables. Finally, though, the dark blue pinstriped, less-than-junior diplomatic type behind the desk gave it to him. He put it into his back pocket and headed back out on the Reforma for the half-mile walk to the Camino Real Hotel.

It was about the best that Guatemala had to offer. Slick, modern, and clean. The bullet holes on the entrance wall from the last coup had been filled in. Entering the lobby, he nodded at one of the two sharp, tough-looking Latin men in severely cut gray suits who were always present by the door. The bulges under their arms did not come from breast implants. He knew them for what they were, and they

knew him also: There was an aura about them that
each could recognize.

He went to the back bar and found a table in the
rear, where he could watch the comings and goings
of the customers, ordered a Gallo, and sipped on it as
he went through the paper.

He found the section Tommy had told him to look
for. Third article, international section. Attempted
assassination of the *comandante* of the ARDE faction
of the Nicaraguan Contras. Was that it? No way to
tell; he'd just have to wait. But if it was the Contras
who wanted him, what for? To train some of their
people as shooters, or to advise them on ways to
keep their boss from getting his ass shot off?

The Camino Real was another type of cultural center for Guatemala. Here was where the money would
come, and the hustlers from outside looking to do
business. He'd tried to sell the army some Hu-1b
military utility-type choppers Tommy had located in
West Germany. They could be bought through a
Swiss company and shipped direct to Puerto Barrios.
But he had no luck. It took nearly a month to find out
why. They just didn't want them. They wanted
H-model Hueys or French Alouettes, which were
capable of getting up to much higher altitudes. Guatemala had mountains and volcanoes going up twelve
thousand feet. The guerrillas could get above the old
B models and throw rocks down on them.

Why couldn't they have just said they didn't want
them instead of wasting his time? Latins had a strange
reluctance to just come flat out and say no. Maybe
they didn't want to hurt your feelings and thought
that after a while—a week, a month, a year—you'd
just go away and save them that kind of embarrass-

ment. It usually worked and was widely known in the trade as the Central American two-step.

The Camino Real had its set of resident characters. *Pensiones* like Old Duff, a retired British civil servant who would show up at three o'clock on Mondays, Thursdays, and Fridays, and sit at the corner of the bar drinking till he couldn't walk, which always occurred before six. He'd be gently escorted by the stocky men in gray suits to a cab and sent home. Those were the only days you'd see him. If you caught him before his mouth stopped working, he'd tell stories of his service in Malaya and China, India and Africa. Sometimes Duff would be met by Paul Frolich, a former Luftwaffe fighter pilot. Tall and distinguished, he was the perfect prototype for an ex-Messerschmidt pilot. He and Duff would refight the war for an hour or two, trading well-known and cherished insults.

The old man had a lot of history. Now he was just drinking himself to death, having stated once that drink was the only civilized way to commit suicide and the most fun.

Rossen hung around until eight-thirty, watching the different types come and go. Distinguished Spanish *dons* with young expensive women on their arms, planters, and mine owners. Mixed in were some military types who tried to look as if they were civilians and never quite succeeded.

Outside, it had turned dark. He nodded at the doorman, who whistled up a taxi from the line waiting at the curb.

It was a '74 Chevy that should have gone to General Motors heaven five years ago. Before getting in he performed the standard ritual of settling the price of the ride first.

"Quanto por el puerto de aereo?"

The driver habitually increased his normal fare by thirty percent.

"Diez quetzales, señor."

Rossen spat back at him, *"Cree usted, yo soy un pendeho turista?"*

The driver didn't care if he was a dumb tourist or not. It still never hurt to ask for more.

"Bueno, señor. Cinco quetzales."

3

As they pulled into the airport, Rossen saw a jet touching down. Should be the one Tommy was on. The cab let him off under the slightly curious gaze of a couple of security police who weren't very interested in the comings or goings of their own people, but figured any foreigners were worthy of at least a second glance, just to see if it made the object of their attentions uneasy. Rossen ignored them and the M-2 carbines they carried from slings on their shoulders, their hands resting on the barrels, the rifles held horizontal to their waists. That seemed to be the accepted manner of carrying the World War II leftovers.

Taking the outside ramp, he went upstairs to where he could look down on the arriving passengers as they filed into the customs lines to have their baggage inspected. He hoped Tommy wouldn't have any trouble. Last week a group of male tourists from Taiwan came in and had the dog shit beat out of them.

The guards, as at many third world airports, were not among the most intelligent in the world, and there had been rumors in the city about North Vietnamese coming into the country to advise the guerrillas. None of the Chinese were seriously hurt, only two had to be hospitalized. Apologies had been made, but the guards were still a bit touchy about Orientals.

Lighting a Marlboro, he leaned on the railing watching the incoming people. Most were families returning from the States, and they had the biggest suitcases he'd ever seen. At the customs counter these were opened. They were filled with what looked like the spoils of a looting raid. Everything from clothes to stereos fell out of them. He could hear one phrase being used over and over, "*Para mi usar personal*," "for my personal use," the speakers trying to avoid the heavy Guatemalan duty on any foreign products brought into the country. He hoped Tommy hadn't brought any firearms with him.

Then he saw him. Traveling light, carrying only two flight bags. Rossen knew that was all he had with him. That was all he ever carried. Tommy looked around, then up to the balcony, and saw Rossen waving at him. He gave a tired grin and headed into the customs line. Setting his bags on the counter, he waited patiently for his turn while a customs official finished inspecting a suitcase that looked like a cargo container for the *Queen Mary*.

Before opening Tommy's flight bags, the officer requested his passport, even though Tommy had just gone through immigration. Watching, Rossen had the feeling that if the passport hadn't been an American one, Tommy might have been in a bit of trouble. Still

suspicious, the inspector went through Tommy's bags
with a fine tooth comb. Finding nothing seemed to
make him even more suspicious—for a moment Rossen
thought the inspector was going to make Tommy
remove his steel claw and have it X-rayed—but he
stamped the bags and waved him through, groaning
at the size of the next bag being put on his counter. It
belonged to a grandmother whose three middle-aged
sons were helping her lift it up.

Heading back down the ramp to the outside, he
met Tommy at the curb. A quick hug on the shoulders and they headed for one of the waiting cabs.
Once more the ritual haggling, and they were on their
way back into town.

Tommy rolled down the window to breathe the
cool night air of the five-thousand-foot-high city. It
felt good.

"Jim, I am a beat man. From Belgium to Paris,
then New York, then Miami, and now here. God, I
wish things would slow down sometimes." He cast
an eye on his friend's face as light from passing cars
and signs flashed over it. "You don't look so good,
buddy. Been in the ink?"

"Well, you know I like just a touch now and
then."

"Yeah, I remember when you didn't drink a quart
of booze in six months and didn't smoke a pack of
butts in a year. You look like shit."

"Thanks a lot, Tommy, that's a real ego booster."

"Fuck your ego. You need to get your act together. Man, you're the best and you can't stay that
way unless you believe it. I got us a good job, but
you're going to have to do the final sell. It's you they
want to see. So clean out your system or we could

blow this one—and they already sent me a deposit. You know how it upsets me to return money.''

Rossen wouldn't have taken that kind of talk from anybody but Tommy. They went back a long way—to a hundred nights spent together on the "hardballs" in 'Nam. Days and nights where one life depended on the other. That was the kind of thing that either made you love the man you were with or hate him. You became more than many who were born brothers.

Tommy scratched the side of his face with his steel hook, then rubbed his wrist with his good hand. Rossen knew that wrist ached all the time. The hand had not been lost to any real act of war; it had been surgically removed by a Viet Cong sniper who used Tommy to bait Rossen into a stupid shootout. The Cong shooter's ego was what finally got him. He wanted to play, and death is not a game where you can get an instant replay.

He knew Tommy was tired, suffering jet lag and the constant nagging pain of his wrist. "We'll just pack it in tonight. You can fill me in on the details tomorrow. You ain't worth a shit right now.''

Tommy didn't answer. A small snore started, then stopped. He was asleep.

Rossen sat in silence all the way back into zone one. It wasn't till they made the turn off Avenida Sexta near the Tejano restaurant that Tommy woke up. One more turn to the left and they pulled up in front of the Ritz Continental. With his unexpected windfall from last night Rossen had paid for the rooms up front.

Tommy gave the desk clerk his passport for registration, took it back, and they headed to the third floor with a porter leading the way, carrying the two

small bags. They left the porter at the door and
Tommy didn't even stop for a quick trip to the john.
He just zeroed in on one of the two beds and went for
it facefirst, mumbling in his pillow, "Call me for
breakfast, but don't do it till lunch," and he was out.
Rossen waited until he was sure he was in a deep
regular sleep, then took Tommy's shoes off and pulled
a cover up over him. They'd get a fresh start in the
morning. It was enough that Tommy was back. He
had missed the little Nisei. That was something that
he didn't used to do.

As Tommy slept, Rossen lay back on his bed and
looked out into the night sky. Lighting up another of
the Honduran-made Marlboros, he wondered, *What
next, and where?* He'd asked that question too
many times.

Looking at Tommy, he saw the steel hook at the
end of his wrist reflecting spots of light from the bulb
left on in the bathroom. He had always felt a bit
guilty because Tommy had lost his hand because of
him. God, that seemed so long ago. 'Nam, Cambo-
dia, Laos: They'd been through it all together. Tommy
was the only one he could talk to that really understood.

What was it they said, it took one to know one.
Not exactly true. Tommy *was* different, less isolated
inside. Even though he was nearly as good a shooter
and had over fifty kills, he didn't strike most people
the same way. *I guess it's just a matter of person-
ality, and Tommy's got more of it than I do.*

There was one other who tried to talk to him once,
tried to understand. What was his name? *Yeah, Asher.
Dr. Sidney Asher.* He'd been the shrink in 'Nam
who was doing the study on snipers so the army
could find more of them. He'd been okay. Rossen

thought that Dr. Asher had learned more than he wanted to about the giving and taking of life. The first rule was snipers didn't give, just took. Add to that the ability to time and again watch a man's head explode in your scope and not go mad or become a kill junkie and get hooked on it: That was the secret.

Sniper! Rossen didn't even like the sound of the word. To most, it was someone who snuck around in alleys or lurked on building tops to shoot some poor soul in the back, then sneak away. He and Tommy had done that. But their targets were not poor souls. He didn't like those jobs either. Only twice had he been handed over to the tender ministrations of the "Company" for special assignment.

Traffic noise outside eased off. Rossen heard the night whistlers. He'd have to ask Freddie about them sometime. He didn't have the faintest idea who they were, but every night, if you listened, you could hear them. Long melodic whistles that were answered with a couple of notes added to them and passed on. Maybe they were just security people guarding the offices and buildings singing to keep each other awake during the long night hours.

He and Tommy had heard singing before. The special singing of fear that came in the night in a thousand forms and sounds. The flutter of a bird's wings or the rustle of a lizard moving through high grass. Each sound magnified and unexpected. His back began to sweat. Fear. He knew it. Tommy knew it. But time and again they went back to taste it. What was there about it that kept drawing them back, made them so they couldn't live like other men with families and jobs? Tommy gave out a small snore.

He butted out the cigarette. Tommy was right. He did smoke and drink too much. He'd have to get his shit together or one day he'd make a mistake and one of them would die. If that happened, he hoped it'd be him instead of Tomanaga. Like old folks who had been married all their lives, each hoped he would die before the other.

His eyes blinked once, twice, then he was out, not knowing when the exact moment of sleep came.

"Roll out, shooter, we got things to do and talk about."

He rolled over and groaned. Tommy was up and showered, looking fresh as a spring flower. Rossen looked like an unmade bed.

"Okay, Tommy, you go on down to the restaurant and get some coffee. I'll clean up and be down in ten minutes."

"Dai jobu, tomadachi," Tommy agreed, and left Rossen to put his appearance back in order.

He found Tommy sitting at a table near the window overlooking an outside garden that represented a small tropical jungle of birds of paradise and other exotic flowers he didn't recognize.

The waitress came over and smiled, handing him the menu.

"Café con leche solamente, por favor."

"Bueno, señor."

Once he had a cup of the thick rich coffee of which the Guatemalans were so rightfully proud, he finally asked, "What's the whole deal?"

"I was contacted in Brussels by an agent for the Contras. They'd gotten our names somewhere and

were looking for us. From what they said, all they
want is a few training cycles to be run through. At
any rate, we needed the work. I lost us the contract
to run that security job for the Belgian 'Minière
Concerne.' That's okay with me though. I'm not
much for central Africa. We never had any good
come out of there.

"So I'm here and we meet the principles in
Tegucigalpa day after tomorrow. The flight's booked
and hotel reservations are made. That's all there is to
it. It came down fast and simple. The hard part was
figuring out which flea bag you'd gone to ground
in."

"Yeah, how'd you locate me? I know you didn't
call Freddie."

Tommy sipped at his steaming aromatic brew. "You
remember General Villatoro? Well, I reached him at
the ministry and he just had his people check on the
passport lists of the different hotels. And there you
were. He still kinda likes you, Rossen, though I
don't know why."

Rossen didn't either. They'd given the general a
bit of a hard time a few years back, but it was more a
philosophical dispute than anything violent. Villatoro
had been proven right in time—maybe that's why he
was so gracious.

Tommy interrupted his train of thought. "Well,"
he began, putting down the cup, "I think I'll make it
now. What say we go over and say hi to Freddie? I'd
like to see him again." He looked down at Rossen's
wrist. "I see he still hasn't got your watch."

They hit the streets for the three-block walk over
to the Europa. As always, the streets were crowded

and moving fast, with the food and sweets vendors doing steady business.

Going up the steps, they were met at the door by Freddie, who was just coming back from his morning run over to the central market where he bought produce fresh from the fields.

"*Hola,* Tomanaga, it's good to see you. Catch the door for me, will you?"

Tommy opened the door to the restaurant, and Freddie went straight back to the kitchen, dropped his load off, and went behind the bar.

"Okay, yesterday he said a friend was coming in. We're the only two I know that could like him, so I was hoping it was you. This calls for a morning drink. How about you, Rossen? Tommy?" Tommy nodded okay. He didn't usually drink this early, but when Freddie offered to buy a drink, it was an occasion.

Rossen thought about Tommy's words last night. "No thanks, Freddie. I think it's time to dry out a bit."

Freddie eyed Tommy, his mustache bristling as he smiled.

"I always knew you were a good influence on this barbarian, Tommy. But I don't see why you put up with him." Tommy started to say something, but Freddie raised his hand.

"I know he's your friend, though God knows why, when you seem to be such a sensible type. You know he's going to get you killed one of these days, don't you? So why don't you just take him home, and you two find wives, get them pregnant, and raise children. You're getting too old for this game."

"Oh, please, Freddie, no lectures. I've traveled

fourteen thousand miles just to see your smiling face, and this is the bullshit I get? I know you're right, you always are, but it doesn't make any difference. Me and Rossen are victims of our own mythology.''

Freddie chewed that one over a bit. Victims of their mythology. A good line. He'd figure it out later.

"Okay, men. No more lectures, but I'll tell you this. I can lease the empty store next to me and triple my business. If you want something steady this time, save your money and become my partners. I make this offer only because my wife insists that I do one good deed a year for the less fortunate.''

Tommy gave Rossen a stern look when Freddie said, ''This time save your money.'' Rossen shook his head. He'd said nothing to him about the job. Freddie caught the look. "Don't get touchy. I'm not completely stupid. He said a friend was coming in and he'd pay his bill today. You're here, that means you two are going to work. It's not like I solved the riddle of the pyramids. Remember, I once had an uncle in the Gestapo. In a way you guys remind me of him. Pains in the ass!''

Tommy grinned sheepishly. "Okay, Freddie, I'm sorry. Now, give me our friend's check and I'll settle up. You do take dollars here, don't you?''

Freddie grunted, mollified. ''Do bears shit in the woods?''

They spent a couple of hours visiting with Freddie, then headed back for the hotel. Dinner that night with two of the good churrasco steaks in the Caverna restaurant. Back to Freddie's for a nightcap, then they hit the sack.

Freddie told them he'd drive them to the airport.

He was a good man and a good friend. He renewed his offer of a partnership. Rossen and Tommy had come to an agreement earlier. If the deal went down right, they'd take him up on his offer, but they knew they wouldn't be working partners. There was no way they'd be able to sit down in one place and wait tables and cook. Besides which, Freddie didn't really need them. But he would make them a profit and they'd always have somewhere to go. That was the most important thing. To have somewhere to go.

4

Sweat beaded up on his forehead, then gathered in pools around the hollows of his eyes. His tunic stuck to his back in the sweltering heat.

For Sergei Rasnovitch this was nearly hell. He didn't know which was worse, Managua in summer or Kabul in winter. Each was totally miserable and filled with ignorant peasants. Careful, he thought, *peasants* is a word we do not use anymore. Filled with ignorant comrade workers. Snorting at his extraordinary sense of humor, he blew his nose. It was well suited for blowing. Large with deep pores and crevices.

His official title was military attaché to the Soviet embassy. On his previous assignment he'd been officially under the Office of Cultural Relations. Culture, he groaned. There is no culture stronger than fear. Fear, hate, and hunger, hunger for power, wealth, money. All the things that one lusts for in his heart, and if he believes in it, in his soul, are the great motivators.

Sergei Rasnovitch loved the USSR. He was totally devoted to it and its concept of the world. He knew there was no other society currently in existence where he could, or would, have been permitted to function in such a manner. He had seen the Panzers of Germany invade his homeland when he was still a child, and he had seen the men he had sent to the Gulags for reeducation. There was one common denominator, fear! He had seen it on the faces of the German storm troopers when they'd been taken prisoner in the tens of thousands. There was fear on the faces of the hundreds of his comrades he had personally interrogated. He loved the feeling of security and confidence it gave him. This was power. True power backed by the strength of the Soviet armed forces. He could indulge his needs in all that he wished as long as he showed results. That was all that mattered, that he show results. And he always had.

Still, it was a bit difficult when he was assigned to these foreign places where the sun beat down like hammers and humidity choked off one's very breath. He hated the tropics, he hated the jungle, and he hated the brown dark-eyed people who lived in them. But for now, if his superiors said they were his brothers, then brothers they would be, and he would smile when it was necessary, laugh when it was called for. He was relieved and grateful for those few precious moments when such unnatural behavior was not called for: when he was demonstrating techniques of interrogation or the different methods of breaking an opponent's confidence.

Some of them were crude but effective. He found

the cruder the method, the faster results were obtained. Oh, yes, he could, with time, make a man betray his own mother and never touch him. That was a good game—to find and let loose the weakness and perversion that lay within the souls of all men, let them loose but on a very thin, exceedingly strong, mental leash. Those were the ones from which he could get the most value.

But it was so hard to impart his wisdom to these Sandinistas. These new Marxists and Socialists. The Cubans were difficult enough, but at least there they had only Castro to deal with. Castro was capable of keeping his subordinates under complete control. Here, everything was done by committee. The more people involved, the more complicated it became. But that was his burden, and he would bear it with the manner of a true stoic.

"God, it is so hot." He longed for the air-conditioned suite that was put at his disposal in what had been the Managua Hilton. It was the only decent facility left in the city. He had his own technicians brought in to keep the hotel equipment running properly, and they didn't always succeed. One thing about the Americans, they could keep air-conditioners running when no one else could. The same thing had happened when the Portuguese left Angola and the French the Congo. When the rebels displaced their masters and took over the country, much of the machinery came to a stop.

The staff car let him off at the entrance to the Revolutionary Office of Internal Affairs. He moved his Afghani camelhide briefcase to his left hand, freeing his right, a habitual act. On either side, his own security men in civilian dress flanked him, their weapons readily accessible but concealed. It was here he was to meet his counterpart, Comrade Luis Guzman. They had much to discuss; lists waited to be drawn of those who required surveillance and those who simply needed to disappear. That was always convenient in these circumstances. One simply claimed they had run off to join the Contras and that was the end of it.

The Sandinista sentries at the door carried new issue weapons, not the leftovers normally supplied to most revolutionary movements. Their boots were shined, their faces brown, bright, and intense. They saluted sharply at his approach. One broke position to open the door for him. Sergei smiled a sweaty red grin with heavy-fleshed lips. One must always be pleasant when dealing with inferiors.

His guards moved to new positions, one to the front, one to the rear. They walked down hallways where once the corrupt officials of Somoza dealt out justice and robbed the country blind. Thank God for petty dictators. They made his work so much easier. He caught himself after the thought and gave his childhood a mental chastising. The Russian Orthodox church did a pretty fair job of indoctrination itself. But then the party was often quite catholic in its approaches to problems and population control. For many, it had simply taken the place of the church. If one had aberrant social thoughts, one went to the local party commissar; he listened, and gave you pamphlets to read instead of Hail Marys. Then, if you were properly contrite, he forgave your errors in the name of the party and put your name on a list for future reference.

Overhead fans turned slowly, barely enough to move the muggy air. Once more he wished for the expertise of the Americans in making things run. Stopping at the alcove where the steps led up to the next floor, he breathed heavily, wiped his face, and checked his buttons. Appearance was so critical. His uniform was spotless, with the order of Suvarov first-class and party badges properly displayed. He would have looked fit for an audience with the Supreme Soviet Presidium if it had not been for the dark sweat spots that had already collected around his armpits and the small of his back. A Sandinista officer passed him heading to the outside. He was typical. Fatigues either dull green or camouflage. Why do all of these people seem to have such a penchant for dressing badly and wearing beards in a climate where even the rocks sweat?

He was in the section where intelligence and state security were determined and analyzed. More sentries stood behind wire-framed, bulletproof glass cages to inspect one's papers before permitting entry. Comrade Colonel Sergei Rasnovitch presented his identification and waited patiently while it was checked against a master list and his face compared with the photographs on file. The sentries knew who he was, but still adhered rigidly to their format. Only once had one of them permitted the Russian entrance without going through the required rituals. His current status in life was now a matter of morbid speculation. Sergei was very insistent about having examples set where matters of security were concerned.

He left his men sitting sullenly behind on straight-back cane chairs as he was permitted inside. Once more he straightened his uniform, cursed the heat, and headed briskly down to the third glass-faced door marked simply 204, where he entered without knocking.

It took only a cursory glance to tell that all was in a state of Latin confusion and disorder. Papers and files were strewn about on desks. Dark-eyed secretaries looked up at his entrance, then quickly hid bottles of American nail polish and increased the tempo of their work. As always, pictures of Sandino, their heroic symbol, decorated most available wall space. The colonel grunted at the thin face under the cowboy hat. Even the semi-deified Lenin wasn't in so much evidence in Russia as Sandino was here. But as he knew, the masses must have their symbols and heroes. Personally, he wished the ARDE *comandante* were still on their side. He was one of the few Nicaraguan leaders with any true charisma. He could have been a major factor in securing their position in Central America, but the man was impossible to deal with.

To Luis's secretary he made a small old-world bow. "Will you announce me to Comrade Guzman please." It was not really said as a question, and she knew it. Rosalia Lopez knew where the real power in her country was, and a good portion of it rested with the fat, red-faced, large-pored Russian. She would have fucked him in a minute if he would have gotten her Luis's job. She knew it and so did he. Hitting the intercom switch, she announced his presence and smiled with large ripe lips.

"Please go right in, Colonel, and have a nice day."

Sergei grinned, eyeing her. Miss Lopez was what most foreigners would think of when they dreamed of hot-eyed, raven-haired, passionate Latin women. Long-legged, with round breasts above a waspish waist,

Miss Lopez was most certainly an asset to any office decor.

"Keep up the good work, señorita. With your attitude, I am sure you will progress rapidly to positions of greater importance." He paused before opening the door to Luis's office. "If you should ever wish to discuss the matter in more detail, I am at your service." It never hurt to keep the hook baited.

He entered and closed the door behind him.

"Good day, Señor Guzman. I have come to discuss a problem or two with you. It seems that our friends on the San Juan are going to try to create a bit of disturbance."

Luis Maria Guzman DeMondragon rose from behind his desk and came around the corner to give his guest a Soviet-style hug and kiss. "Welcome, Sergei. What is this about trouble? Don't we have enough without you digging up new ones all the time?"

Sergei settled heavily into an overstuffed leather chair, sighing with relief as he transferred the burden of his bulk from his legs to the cushions. Casually, he surveyed his host as he always did. Señor Guzman was of average appearance, not over five foot ten, one hundred forty-five pounds, black hair, brown eyes. Not bad-looking, and young enough to still have ideas. He would be twenty-seven in four months. *Perhaps he'd be twenty-seven.*

"True, Comrade Luis. Very true. However, we still have our troublesome friend and former comrade to the south. So far we have been fairly successful in keeping him from obtaining too much American aid, and he stubbornly refuses to come to any kind of an agreement where he'd have to take orders from the Americans or the FDN. All that is to our immediate advantage. The *comandante* as of this time is the only one among the Contra leaders who could rally much popular support."

He stopped to collect his thoughts, motioning for Luis to regain his seat behind his desk before continuing.

"The *comandante* must die. I have read with great dis-ap-point-ment"—he stretched the word out, —"the results of your last attempt to terminate this irritant. I do wish that I was permitted to use our own people for the job; it would be done then, quickly, efficiently, and be over with. But Moscow has in its infinite wisdom determined that no citizen of the Soviet Union or its European allies be involved directly in the assassination. It is therefore once again back to you. And I would suggest that you come up with a plan that will succeed while you are still capable of doing so."

Luis felt his heart skip a beat, his chest suddenly growing much tighter.

Sergei knew the reaction his words had created. Leaning forward to rest his elbows on his knees, he gazed at Luis with his pale, nearly washed-out eyes, set deep in lids that had just a touch of Mongolia to them.

"No, my friend. Your danger comes not from us, your comrades. Rest easy on that score; you are truly appreciated by us and we have great things in mind for you.

"No! Your troubles will not come from us. However, you should be prepared to take more precautions. It appears that our unsuccessful efforts to terminate the *comandante* have created undesirable results. Topo, your counterpart with the *comandante*, has taken a leaf from your book. We have word that he has sent for an American assassin. A specialist who is not connected with the CIA or any other official American agency. All that we know is that he is an accomplished and successful killer. That and no more is known at this time: He is just a killer. We have no name or any other information. But once he has reached the zone, we'll know who he is. Possibly before then. There are only so many ways for him to come in. Our people in Honduras and Costa Rica will be especially watchful for new faces. But there is no guarantee that he will be spotted in time.

"Therefore, until we have him located and identified, I would suggest that you stay within the borders of your own country and not give him an opportunity to get at you where we are not able to control the security situation properly. If he wants you, then we shall make him come to us here."

Luis had the sudden and unpleasant feeling that someone was watching him. He did not like it. Before, when they had fought the Somozas, it had been different. He'd been with his comrades in the jungle, supported by them. He had been able to face his enemies directly. Now he'd been told that someone was coming to kill him. Someone he didn't know. Someone that was an expert. He felt very vulnerable. In his current job he knew how difficult it was to be protected every second of every day when the assassin could strike at any moment with any weapon. Poison, rocket attack, bombs? For the first time he began to appreciate the word *terror*. It was not good.

His back stuck to the leather seat of his chair.

"But Comrade Colonel, would it not be better if I took the flight this Saturday to Havana? There it would be much more difficult for the assassin to reach me." He was speaking of the weekly flight to Havana that carried diplomats, classified mail pouches, and sometimes people for special training.

Rasnovitch did not smile. His voice lowered to where it was barely perceptible.

"No, Comrade Guzman. You will not go to Cuba. You will stay here and do your job. I want this man. If he is an American, we can use him to great effect in our propaganda efforts. If at all possible, I would like to take him alive. He could be very important to us." Sergei grinned, showing strong yellow front teeth. "You know, it is within the realm of possibility that he could be even more important than you are. Isn't that an amusing thought?"

5

Topo Bustamante hung up the receiver with deliberateness and ran his hands through his thinning hair. He looked older than his thirty-eight years; the last few years had been hard ones. Getting the resistance organized, funding, communications, propaganda, settling squabbles among the different elements who supported them so none felt slighted. All took time and all took money, which was in short supply. Lately, the CIA station agent in Costa Rica had been a bit difficult to deal with, and there were threats of the agency cutting off all their funds and supplies if the *comandante* did not come to a rapprochement with the FDN in the north, who were working out of bases in Honduras. It was a most trying job. Rising from his seat, he walked to the window and looked out. He could see the tall buildings of the downtown area of San José. It was a beautiful city, the people friendly, the climate mild. But the Costa Ricans were feeling pressure, too.

In the last two weeks there had been two border incidents with the Sandinistas, and the Costa Ricans were not noted for having a warlike attitude. They had tried for millennia. A nation without an army and not much of a national police force. No tanks, no fighter planes, not even any artillery. A tropical version of Switzerland.

The pressure from the Sandinistas on the Costa Ricans to deny the rebels sanctuary was growing very strong, and they were afraid of being sucked up into the war. If the Contras hadn't been better armed than the national police, they might have tried to do more, not just make an occasional raid and confiscate a few weapons and radios every now and then.

Problems. Always problems. Now there had been another attempt on the *comandante*'s life. The third one in the last four months. A bomb attack at their headquarters on the Nica side of the Rio San Juan. The explosion was heard at the trading post where the San Juan merged with the San Carlos River two miles away. The worst of it was that the bomb went off during a press interview and an American female journalist had been killed along with three soldiers. The assassin was an agent of the Sandinistas, posing as a foreign *periodista*. The *comandante* had been lucky, again. This had to be stopped. Without the *comandante*, the morale of the fighters would turn to shit, and even if the man were a bit narrow-minded and suffered from political tunnel vision, he was the one that held the revolution together.

There had been many meetings with the leaders of the Revolutionary Alliance, and it had been decided to fight fire with fire.

Topo had been lucky. Already working for them as

a *voluntario,* not even taking any pay, was a Vietnam veteran his peoples' children called Papa Gringo. He was a former medico with the American La Forca Especial, las Boinas Verde, the Green Berets, who was running a dispensary for refugee children. From him they had learned of this Rossen and had been given a number in Georgia to call. Then they had been given the name of the man who had been Rossen's partner and was in Belgium. They had an agent in France who had been trying to buy arms. He was put in contact with the Oriental, who then called his comrade and set the meeting in two days in Tegucigalpa, Honduras. They were exactly the kind of personnel he required. He had thought it would be more difficult to find a man or group of men who could be trusted to perform a sensitive and surgical operation. He didn't want to use a bomb. Bombs did not care who they killed. Guilty and innocent alike were taken. *No!* He was not a barbarian. He wanted someone who would kill selectively with good taste and judgment. There were not many around with the qualifications he required available on the open market. This time he had been lucky. Now he was thinking of a way to make them even more effective, and of course, there was the El Salvadoran situation. He would have to contact Georges and see if his proposition was still open.

It had been surprisingly simple to locate them. Once he had the names, he contacted his agents in Miami and set them to work on finding out all they could about the two men. It was not difficult: They had friends in the American military establishment who wished them well, even if the CIA was giving them a hard time. These two men, this Oriental

Tomanaga and the other—what did Papa Gringo call them?—this other, "shooter," Jim Rossen, were more than qualified. Officially, Rossen had over a hundred kills to his credit, and Tomanaga nearly half that. They would do . . . and they were looking for work. Topo liked that. Men who had fought the Communists in other parts of the world were to his liking. It increased the odds of their being on his side of the war emotionally, if not always politically. He wanted men like these, who had lost friends to the Communists and had seen the results of the enemy's handiwork at first hand. It simplified many things. Made it easier.

Topo lit a Delta and inhaled. Of course, he would have to ease the gringo into the profile he wished. Just to be certain. Let them get involved with the people. Be treated as friends, see the wounded and crippled children, the starving campesinos and Indians who had been forced from their homes. Let them get involved a bit at a time; then, when they were ready, he would use them to kill. There were several on the list, including a Cuban and a Russian, but more than them he wanted this shooter to kill Comrade Luis Maria Guzman DeMondragon, Topo's counterpart in the Sandino hierarchy. It was he who had ordered the attempts on the *comandante*'s life, and it was he who would soon be terminated, as the CIA men like to say. Terminated with extreme prejudice. What a lot of words just to say you are going to have someone killed. *Estúpido!*

He looked back at his desk, at the pile of paperwork awaiting his attention, and groaned inwardly. He wished he could have been back at the university teaching agronomics instead of trying to keep his current associates in a harmonic and constructive mood. He was a Latin, but his grandmother had been German and he looked more like her side of the family. Nearly six foot three with gray-green eyes and a complexion that did not do well in the sun. But his heart was that of a Nica, and so he was here doing what he could. The Sandinistas had to go, or his country would be no more than another Cuba still dangling from a string, but it would be Russia's then, and not America's. If there were a choice between strings, he'd have to pick the gringos.

He looked up at the flag of the revolution, a blue and white striped banner with the initials of the revolutionary movement embroidered upon it in gold. Symbols and money! He often wondered which was the more important, and decided rapidly to stay with money. With it one could buy plenty of symbols. Or have them manufactured.

Picking up the phone, he hit the intercom button for the secretary downstairs.

"Find Juliano and send him to me." He had thought about Rosalia. Nice bottom, high firm breasts . . . but the Smith and Wesson 9mm she wore on her hip with such determination put a damper on his ardor. Female fanatics are the worst kind. It had been so long since she'd had any, it would probably need dusting. He thought about using the only certain ploy he could come up with to bring her to her knees: She was the type who, if she thought for a second it would help the cause, would screw the entire country of Honduras. But, then, Honduras was not all that big.

If she thought a night with Topo would ease his mind of strain and make him more functional, she would do it in a heartbeat. It was tempting, until the memory of the gun crept in again. Three years ago he had seen her shoot a man in Managua, and her target was between his legs.

Involuntarily, he shuddered. No! She was better off where she was. At a desk, doing her job, and being a devoted fanatic. Also, she still had relatives in Managua and they were nearly as fanatical as she was.

He would save her for another use, another time, when she might have more value than simply easing some of his internal pressures.

He passed the next few minutes going over the budget. There was never enough. Their small but vital air force consisted of a few propellor-driven private planes and a couple of old Loach helicopters which were constantly overloaded, thereby putting enormous strain on their motors and frames. Petrol was stored in anything they could find, including old fifty-five-gallon paraguat tanks. He had never found out where they came from, but the paraguat residue had caused continuing problems with the helicopter's fuel. Now he'd had to go to the additional expense of hiring two full-time American helicopter mechanics to work on them. He had another expert coming from Guatemala to assist them for a couple of weeks, a master mechanic who had served in the American armed forces but was Guatemalan by birth and nationality. He had hoped to find someone among his people who had the ability to be trained in basic maintenance, but it had been futile. Now he had to pay for outsiders to come in and keep their machines in the air.

Juliano was the best of his pilots. Soon he would

be promoted to the rank of commander, with an
entire region under his command. Quick, bright,
young, and well-educated, he knew his job, having
flown first for the Somozas then defecting to the
Sandinistas, then defecting again when he became
disillusioned with them. When he came back to serve
once more with the *comandante*, he brought a plane
belonging to the Sandinistas with him.

Rosalia found Juliano in the radio room speaking
to one of the American helicopter mechanics, nodding his head in understanding and disgust as he
wrote down their shopping list of parts. Signing off,
he acknowledged Rosalia's presence with a nod and
eyed her well-rounded buttocks.
   "Yes, Rosalia, what is it?"
   "Topo wishes for you to come to his office."
   "*Bueno*. I want to talk to him also."
Juliano had a great deal of respect for Topo and
appreciated his difficulties. But he could concern
himself with only those problems for which he had
direct responsibility: Keeping the aircraft in the air
and not on the ground, where they did no one any
good. He left Rosalia at her desk and speculated on
the possibilities that lay behind her permanently pout-
ing upper lip. Fascinating! But was she worth the
aggravation that would follow if she decided she was
in love with you? He, too, recalled the ball-busting
incident in Managua. That single action gave her
more protection than a Kevlar bullet-proof vest. There
were few among the Contras who would risk the
consequences of her affections. The man she had
shot had been her lover. Now he could sing alto in

any boys' choir anywhere in the world. Since then she had transferred her passions to the rebellion.

He took the steps up to Topo's office two at a time and entered without knocking.

His jefe rose to greet him. "Sit down, compadre. I have something to tell you that I believe will please you. For some time now you have been nagging me to stop being the nice guy and fight the war without restraints."

Juliano leaned forward, his eyes brightening.

"Yes . . . ?"

"You will come with me to Tegucigalpa. There we will meet a couple of American specialists who are not on the payroll of the CIA. I want you with me because of your understanding of these people and their language. You will be my liaison with them. If things work out as I plan, we will cause much grief for the two thorns in our sides. Possibly their removal."

Juliano felt the excitement building in him. At last they were going to take some affirmative actions. "Will that removal also include a fat Russian?"

Topo grinned widely. "That is certainly high on our lists of priorities. As to the actual methods we will use to achieve our goals, they will have to be determined after more consultation and planning. But I may tell you this. The two we have found are most eminently qualified for the job I have in mind."

Juliano left work that day feeling better than he had in years. The plan Topo had would not end the war, but it would have a devastating effect on the morale of the Sandinista leadership. He knew they understood the effects of selective terror. Soon it would be their turn to go nights without sleep, to look over their shoulders at every turn, to watch every car that approached them, fearful that each new face might be that of the one who was sent to kill them. That would please him greatly. And then there was Sergei Rasnovitch.

He had met him while attending Patrice Lumumba University in Moscow. There are times when one instinctively hates another. This was the feeling he had for the Russian. But there was more, reasons that finally completed his disenchantment with the Sandinista movement and forced his defection. No matter what brave and sensitive ideologies were espoused, Nicaragua was his country and the people his people. Many of the things that were being done to them came at the orders of this Russian, who had even less sentiment for the welfare of Nicaragua than did the Americans who supported Somoza for so many years. He wondered what Sergei Rasnovitch would feel like when he found out that he, too, was a target. He had no doubt that the secret of the American assassins would leak out. He gave his enemy that much credit. It was a fact that their headquarters were infiltrated by agents and Sandinista sympathizers. Now they could use it to their benefit.

He was looking forward to meeting their new tools in Tegucigalpa. Topo had finally come to his senses and realized this was not a time for diplomacy and public relations programs. This was a time for killing. Killings that were, to his thinking, long overdue.

6

The flight from Guatemala made one stop. San Pedro Sula brought a feeling of *déjà vu*: small runway, touching down between rows of palms; firing pits, light and heavy machine-gun bunkers placed at critical junctions around the field. On the left as they taxied in were several Hu-1b military utility helicopters and an assortment of other military craft, including two of the old reliable C-47s. The terminal looked more like a Trailways depot in Outcast, New Mexico. They didn't disembark; the plane stayed on the ground only long enough to exchange a number of passengers, then took off for Tegucigalpa. They flew over a range of hills and mountains where roads were few and far between. Someone had said once that Honduras was like a map that had been crumpled up then thrown on the floor to open, and that's the way it looked from the window of the plane. Very rugged country, with many areas where the Indians had not had any contact with civilization for years

57

and didn't want any. Rivers and valleys that didn't appear on anyone's maps were common. In the hills and jungles were mines the Spaniards had worked. Some claims were still worked by hand by the descendants of the original Indian slave laborers who had toiled under the cold eyes of the conquistadores. Other mines were long covered up by the jungle and lost. To the east was the infamous mosquito coast. Swamps and marshes, tropical rains and decay. Towns and villages that hadn't changed in decades. Dirt roads capable of carrying motorized traffic ran only to and from places of work, and the city limits marked the end of electrical supply. The power was created by diesel generators that ran from three to four hours a day, then were shut down till the next day.

To the west was El Salvador, a little better off economically than Honduras, but not much. Honduras and El Salvador had not always been the best of friends: They'd even gone to war over the outcome of a soccer game. People in the States think they are fanatics about football—here, the referees have to be brought in and taken out of the stadiums in armored cars. And wear bulletproof vests on the field.

Most of the other passengers were what would be expected for a flight of this kind. Businessmen traveling around the tropics hawking their wares, a couple of teenage girls probably on their way to school in Tegucigalpa. Two of the other passengers were typical of more recent arrivals on the scene: Yankees in badly fitting suits and sporting short-cropped hair. Professional military was written all over them. From the way they moved and their age, Rossen figured one officer-type and one young sergeant. They had

eyed Tommy and him speculatively when they'd
boarded. He avoided their direct eye contact and
went back to looking out the window. He knew
they'd seen something in him, too, that was familiar.
Rossen smiled: Maybe he reminded them of one of
their DIs in boot camp.

Losing himself in the banks of clouds that rolled
passed the window, his first indication that they were
near their destination came with the *ding* of the No
Smoking sign and the warning to fasten seat belts.
They began their descent. From his window he could
see they were flying low over a ridge of mountains
forming the basin in which Tegucigalpa lay. It was
almost like a strafing pass: the 724 cleared the mountain rim by only a few hundred feet, then dropped
another thousand rapidly, putting it on the glide path
to the airfield. Turbulence gave his stomach a jerk
and accented the squeal of the landing gear being put
down. Then a bump, another one, a slight third, and
they were on the strip rolling, the pilot braking as
much as he could, turbines whining in reverse, and
the plane slowed to a fast walk and turned onto the
ramp leading to the airport.

It looked like a slightly larger version of what he'd
seen at San Pedro Sula. It wasn't impressive, just a
two-story structure that might have served any mid-
sized city in the States. As the plane shuddered to a
full stop, Rossen waited while the rest of the passengers went through the shuffle of trying to get their
luggage out of the overhead and then stood crowded
together until the door opened and they were invited
to get off. Tommy was near the front and already on
his feet. Rossen waited. He was in no hurry—the city
wasn't going anywhere.

He followed the last of the passengers down the ramp and walked over to the immigration counter. There was a lot less security here than he'd seen in Guatemala. The atmosphere was more casual, with no signs of any real tension. Slack. They passed through immigration, paying the small fee for the privilege of setting foot in Honduras, and then claimed their baggage after a cursory inspection. The customs official had spotted him immediately and did some quick mental gymnastics. He prided himself on his ability to spot people and their real professions immediately. The tall gringo in front of the Oriental was a CIA man. That was clear. And as his country was much dependent upon the good will of the USA, he bobbed his head in recognition and quickly stamped Rossen's bags, passing him through. That's how Rossen played it in his mind, anyway. Tommy, however, was being held up, his passport examined closely by two officials. He reentered the customs area and pointed at Tommy.

"He's with me," he said to the man who had passed him through.

The customs officer yelled across to the others, who looked at Tommy, then at Rossen, and then handed back Tommy's papers and waved him on with no further trouble. The customs officer was pleased with himself; he'd been right in his judgment, had spotted another of those CIA gringos who were coming and going through his country with such regularity.

The view during the cab ride into the downtown area reminded Rossen and Tommy of parts of New Mexico, but with palm trees. They checked into the Holiday Inn near the central square, and went directly to their room. Rossen had almost forgotten what a gringo hotel looked and felt like. There was hot water and an air-conditioner and TV with English-language programs. Incredible. Tommy headed for the shower, and Rossen turned the window unit on to Freeze as he stripped to the waist. The phone rang before he was able to lie down on the bed.

"*Sí?*"

"Señor Rossen, I hope you had a good flight. If it is convenient, we should like to meet you and your associate at the Hotel Prado across the square. Room 302 at eight o'clock this evening. Would that be agreeable?"

"Yeah, no problem. We'll see you at eight."

"Till later then, señores. I do think it would be wise to stay close to your rooms in the event there are any changes in our schedule. *Hasta la noche.*"

The voice on the other end had spoken good English with no more accent than some of the Mexican kids he'd gone to school with. There was just a slight back flavor to the pronunciation that said "Spanish."

Stay close to the room? That could have been a warning that they were being watched, but he didn't think so. It was too early in the game for them to have attracted more than the normal attention any foreigners received. But they were paying for the trip, so he'd play it their way.

When Tommy came out of the shower, Rossen told him about the time and place for the meeting.

"Okay with me. I think I'll just crap out until it's time to go."

Having nothing better to do, Rossen followed suit, enjoying the incredible luxury of crisp sheets after a hot shower and sleeping in a chilled room.

* * *

The walk across the square two blocks away from
their hotel was uneventful. There weren't as many
people on the streets as there had been in Guatemala,
and Rossen saw fewer armed men on patrol. The
square got busier as they passed the statue celebrating
the defeat of William Walker, an American adven-
turer who took over a good portion of Central America in the late 1800s. They followed the desk clerk's
directions and found the Prado. They had taken a
couple of precautions in their approach, but couldn't
tell if anyone was on their ass or not. Taking the
elevator, they went up to the designated room. Rossen
checked his watch and waited a few seconds, then
knocked. He did like to be punctual.

As the door to Room 302 opened, someone across
the hall cracked the door to his room a bit.

"Señores Rossen and Tomanaga, please come in."

Entering the room, Rossen spoke to the man whose
voice he'd first heard on the phone. "You know
there's someone across the hall watching us?"

"Yes, we know. They're with us, part of our
security to make certain that we have no unwelcome
visitors. Please come in and be at ease. May I intro-
duce you to Topo, my commander. You may call me
Juliano."

He showed Tommy and Rossen to a couch where
coffee waited for them. Topo moved his chair closer.

"Gentlemen, I am very glad that we have this
opportunity to meet. I presume you know what our
desires are?"

Tommy spoke up. "From what I was told, you
wanted some instructors."

Topo nodded in agreement. "Exactly. We have no shortage of courage among our men, but there is a sad lack of expertise. We would like to come to an agreement where you would come and train some instructors for us, that we could then pass on your skills to the rest of our men."

Tommy looked at Rossen, received the unspoken okay, and took over the conversation. He usually handled business matters.

"To do that would require a training program of five or six weeks with no more than ten men to a class. I think at this time we would agree to run at least three classes through for . . . fifteen thousand dollars American, paid half in front, the balance weekly till the contract is completed."

Rossen nodded his approval. His half would last him six months if he didn't blow it.

Juliano and Topo watched them closely. Rising from his chair, Topo stood beside Juliano, and they spoke softly for a moment.

"Gentlemen," Topo began, "I think we can agree to that. However, I do believe you will not find it an unreasonable request to have you demonstrate some of your skills to us before making a final commitment. If you do that, then I am prepared to make your initial payment immediately."

Neither Tommy nor Rossen was surprised by the request. Like the man said, it wasn't unreasonable.

Tommy picked up the conversation. "That's okay with us. But where do we hold the demonstration?"

Juliano poured a cup of coffee, offering some to his guests, who refused.

"If you will not think us presumptuous, we anticipated this condition and have made arrangements for exactly that. It will be done here in Honduras. Return here at nine o'clock tomorrow morning and we will go to where you'll have what you need. If I am correct, once this is done and the advance payment is made, you are prepared to begin work immediately? It is very important to us. We're badly outnumbered and to compensate we must make our men the best soldiers we can.''

Sensing the interview was at an end, Rossen and Tommy rose.

Rossen stretched out his hand. "You understand right. We can start work immediately. And to tell you the truth, I'm looking forward to it. If you've done your homework, as I expect you have, you know that Tommy and I won't work for just anybody, no matter what the pay. We're on your side in this fight, and will give you our best."

Topo came to them and shook their hands, ignoring Tommy's steel hook.

"Thank you, compadres. We know you will do just that. Until tomorrow then. Oh, by the way. I would appreciate it if you did stay close to your room. We have arranged for security to keep an eye on you there. If you go out onto the streets or visit any of the nightclubs, it would make their job more difficult. You are very important to us. More than you would guess.''

Taking his hand from the doorknob, Rossen turned back. "Do you think we're under surveillance?"

Topo grunted, making a who-knows gesture with his hands.

"It is always possible. It is only that we wish to take what precautions we may. You are, of course, free men and may do or go anywhere you wish. I am only making a request. It is not an order.''

Rossen liked that. ''That's a good point to remember, gentlemen. You can give us requests, but we don't take orders till we're on the job. We'll be here at 0900 hours in the morning. Good night.''

Tommy followed him from the room and back down the hallway to the elevator. They ignored the still-cracked door where Topo's men kept an eye on the hallway. This time when they left the lobby and hit the street, they saw they had picked up two ordinary-looking men. Ordinary in size and dress, that is, but very tough in their body language and eyes. Topo's insurance plan at work. They didn't try to shake them. Tonight they would do as they'd been asked and stay in. Their potential employers were right in what they requested. Even if he and Tommy weren't tailed from Guatemala, it was always possible that Topo and what's his name—Juliano?—had been when they'd come in. They'd wait and see what the next day would bring.

7

Topo Bustamante made two calls, finished them, and lay back on his bed, satisfied. "We're ready. Our friends have their security for the night in rooms to either side of them, and Georges will be here in the morning to take us and our new allies to his mine in the hills, where we will see if they are truly what we require. How do you personally feel about them, Juliano? Are you comfortable with them?"

Juliano poured another cup of the thick rich coffee and sipped a moment. "Yes, if they perform as I expect them to. I think you made the right choice. Do you foresee any problems in getting them to participate in the rest of our venture?"

Topo ran a hand through his thinning hair and settled back, contented, into his pillow.

"My friend, the most difficult part of any game is getting the right players involved. Give our friends a little time, and we will put them to the real job soon enough. You know, there may be one other piece of business we may be able to use them for. We will discuss that with Georges tomorrow. Till then I believe we should do as we recommended for our friends and go to bed early. It is still best not to attract any attention, and our enemies have too many eyes in this city.''

"What do you think of them, Jim?"

"It's too early to tell. For right now they seem okay. But we'll know more later. Tell you the truth, I'm ready to go to work. I've been sitting around on my ass too long." Rossen picked up the phone and dialed room service. "What do you want to eat? Might as well go for the best; they're paying for it.''

The next morning found them on their way into the hills to the north of Tegucigalpa. Their driver was Georges Julliard. In his late twenties, he was ruggedly handsome, with fair hair and light gray-blue eyes. His parents were Swiss, but he'd been born in Peru. His father, a mining engineer, had passed on the family interest in mines and precious metals to his son, who was taking his party to his mine, where he had a silver claim being worked. They went up into a range of dry hills which looked almost desert-like. Surprising, when just over the range of mountains to the east it was subtropical. The spine of mountains that ran down through Central America made the western side dry and the eastern side wet. Twice they passed patrols making sweeps on either side of the road. Finally, they left the main highway and headed off on a dirt road. An hour of twisting,

bumping, and shifting gears brought them to the edge
of the ridge, where they could look down and see
Georges's claim. It was like most of the mines in the
country, an open-pit operation. He kept about a hundred
workers employed full-time.

Georges pointed out the borders of his land.

"This is my last mine. I have been kicked out of
Peru and Chile. I lost a good working gold mine in
El Salvador because the guerrillas moved in and took
it. But they didn't get what they came for. At least I
cheated them out of that." He didn't expand any on
what he'd meant by "cheated," and Rossen knew
that he wasn't going to at this time. But it was a
curious statement.

Climbing back into the Land Cruiser, Georges started
down a long steep grade that led them to a group of
shacks behind a barbed wire barrier manned by tough-
looking Indian guards. Here was the cook's hut, the
mine office, and storage buildings. Rossen and Tommy
saw that the entire area was under observation. Armed
men watched their approach all along the way down.

Georges pulled up in the front of his office and put
the hand brake on. Before getting out, he turned to
face Rossen and Tommy. "The men you saw are my
own security people. They are better armed, if I may
say so, than the regular army here. If I lose this
mine, it's not going to be done without a fight. I
have fifty men under arms and half of the work force
is trained to shoot. This time if they try to kick me
out, someone is going to pay in blood for the effort. I
run no more."

From the shack that served as his office, two men
came out, each wearing a mixture of khaki and olive
drab.

Georges got out of the vehicle and spoke to them a minute. They nodded and went back inside the shack. While they were gone, the rest of them climbed out to stretch their legs.

"I told them to get a couple of rifles for you. Good ones." Tommy and Rossen went to where they could get a look down into the pit. Men were loading bags of earth on their backs and carrying them to where they could be processed through a portable smelter.

The two men Georges had spoken to came out of the shack carrying some magazines and two rifles, a German HK 7.62mm assault rifle and an FN in the same caliber. Both were brand new weapons.

"Will these be satisfactory?"

Rossen took the HK. With no wasted motion he checked the weapon while Tommy did the same with the Belgian FN. Both were in mint condition.

"Yeah, these will do all right. Where do we go to shoot?"

Georges pointed to a rock- and boulder-covered field about five hundred meters long to the west of the shack.

"There, but wait a moment and I'll have one of my men tell the others that there will be some shooting going on and it's all right." He spoke in rapid Spanish, giving his orders. One of the men went to the edge of the pit with a walkie-talkie and began speaking. Across the pit, Rossen could see another armed man responding to what was being said. The first man went back into the hut and came out with some man-sized silhouette targets and began heading out to the clearing.

As they followed him, Georges said, "This is

where we do most of our shooting. We have some stands for the targets to be set up at one, two, and three hundred meters.''

Rossen and Tommy dry-fired the weapons a couple of times to get the feel of the trigger pull. Like most HKs, it was a bit stiffer than Rossen liked, but he could live with it. The FN was just a hair the better weapon, and he knew Tommy liked them. When Georges's man returned from setting up the targets, they both took the one at one hundred meters for their first shots. Each fired from the prone, putting three rounds each in the respective targets, then rose to check them out. They had been aiming for heart shots; Rossen's were a bit high and to the right, Tommy's were just a finger width low.

Returning to their places, they made what adjustments they could and nodded at Juliano and Topo. ''Okay, have your man go back out and set out four more targets at the five-hundred-meter mark. Then we'll shoot.''

Georges looked at Topo, who nodded. Five hundred meters would be a good shot for open-sight rifles. Nothing extraordinary, any decent marksman should be able to hit the target at that distance.

It took a couple of minutes before the new targets were set, and when Georges's man returned, Rossen went to the right of what would be their firing line, Tommy to the left, his claw twisted in the rifle strap of the FN for support. The targets on the range were staggered. Each man would have two targets at each hundred-meter mark, leading to two more at five hundred.

Once they were in position, they backed off twenty paces.

Juliano and Topo moved out of the way to stand with Georges, wondering what the gringos were doing. Tomanaga looked at Rossen, received a nod, and then they moved. Each fired four rounds from the hip at their first two targets, then ran forward, went into a tumbling roll, came up into the kneeling position, and took four more rapid shots. On their feet once more, they shoulder-rolled to the prone and each took eight shots at rapid fire.

The echoes of gunfire rolled off the hills. The entire demonstration had taken less than thirty seconds and sixteen rounds were fired.

Rising, they dusted off their clothes and started down range. Halting, Rossen called back, "You guys gonna come and see if we're worth hiring?"

All targets on the hundred-meter mark had two rounds each in the chest area. Topo looked at Juliano. Nothing very spectacular. The next two targets had the same hits, as did the third set. Topo was disappointed; he had expected something more than just body hits. Rossen and Tommy smiled at each other.

"Don't look so down in the mouth, boys, there's one more set."

When they reached the five-hundred-meter mark, Topo was satisfied. There were no body shots. Each of the four targets had two rounds each dead center in the face.

"Most excellent shooting for open sights. Gentlemen, my congratulations. We have a deal."

Georges just stood there with his man and looked at the targets. If these men could do that with the naked eye, what were they capable of with telescopic sights? He began to believe the story that Rossen had killed over one hundred men and that his Japanese partner had at least half that number to his score.

Georges had his chief guard show Tommy and Rossen around the mine while he talked to Topo and Juliano.

Georges was ecstatic. "When do you think we can get started? I have waited long enough; I want what is mine. I told you a year ago what I would do for you if you could help me, and now we have what we need. With those men we can do it. I know we can!"

Topo touched Georges's shoulder in sympathy.

"I know, my friend. But it is not yet time. There are a few things to be done first. But it will not be long. I have had reports on these two. They are not just hired assassins. We must first do as I have said to Juliano and get them emotionally and psychologically involved with us. When that is done, then we will act on your problem, and believe me, I will not waste a day. You know our needs in this matter are as great as yours. Give me a month or two, then I think we will be ready. Until then, say nothing, do nothing, that could betray us. We will have most likely only this one opportunity. If we fail in the first attempt, the second will be even more difficult. Let us not rush things."

Georges was still anxious, but he understood. It was just that now, for the first time, he saw the chance to do something positive, and it was hard to wait.

"Very well, Topo. I will wait. It seems I have no choice. But remember, every day that we do not move increases our risk."

"I will, my friend. Now, let me get our *tiradores*, our shooters, and go. I have work for them."

Juliano called to them to come back up out of the pits to the Land Cruiser. It was time to go back to Tegucigalpa.

Tommy and Rossen left the mine happy that they weren't in that line of work. Each of the workers carried a forty-pound bag of ore up a half-mile hill and dumped it. Their pay was three dollars a day. High wages for general labor. The route back to Tegucigalpa was the same for about half the distance, then Georges took a side road that would bring them in from a different direction. Rossen knew what he was doing. It was a good practice to vary your patterns. It couldn't hurt and might save your life.

Once they were in the downtown area they saw the Holiday Inn, but went right past it.

"Hey, Topo, aren't we going to the hotel?"

"Not that one, my friend. I arranged for your effects to be taken to a new location, a smaller place at the edge of the city. Just a precaution. There we will settle our business. Then I shall leave to arrange things for your arrival in Costa Rica the day after tomorrow and for your transport from there to the frontier."

Georges pulled into a walled courtyard, where the gate was closed behind them by a sullen-looking campesino with a well-used machete at his side and a carbine on his shoulder.

They were taken to one of the rooms and left at the door.

"Your things are inside. It is not as comfortable as your previous habitation, but it will be only for a short time. I will see you next on the zone."

Tommy started to interrupt him. "Don't we have . . . ?"

Topo smiled and reached out to Juliano, who put a well-stuffed envelope into his hand. "I think it is what you were expecting. I would suggest that you take time to get a safety-deposit box before leaving Tegucigalpa. I recommend Lloyds Bank. Inside you will also find your plane tickets and room reservations for San José. You should have no trouble passing through immigration. Till we meet again. *Vayan con Dios, amigos.*"

Topo and Juliano went with Georges, leaving them standing in front of the room while the dour-looking man with the machete gave them fish-eye stares. Tommy mumbled something about the man looking like a refugee from an old Pancho Villa movie and opened the door to their new quarters. It was as Topo had said, and more what Rossen had gotten used to in the last couple of months. He was kind of glad to be out of the gringo hotel. He didn't really feel very comfortable there. It was too sterile. Squashing a bee-tle the size of a dachshund puppy with his boot heel, Rossen liked the fact that this room definitely had the lived-in feel to it.

8

It went as Topo had said it would. They were met in front of the immigration counter by a rep from the tourist agency who wore a round bright yellow sign the size of a small shield dangling from a chain on his neck, which announced to the world that he was the official representative of Golden Sun Tours. In his hand he held another sign with the names of Rossen and Tommy on it. They passed by the customs inspector with no problems. The agent merely said they were with his tour, and the customs inspector waved them by.

Loading into a Japanese minibus, a *camionetta*, the guide kept up a running spiel all the way into the city, describing Costa Rica's history and culture. He also advised them that if they wished, there were other tours to be had with a discount, as they were already booked into the hotel through their agency and were entitled to a discount on their jungle boat trip and a chance to see the Irazú volcano. To Rossen,

Irazú looked like a molehill compared with the ones in Guatemala. The temperature was about the same as Tegucigalpa but more humid, and air-conditioned cars were scarce. Rossen sat quietly through the half-hour trip to town. At the junction coming onto the main highway from the airport he saw a sign on which was painted the word NICARAGUA with an arrow pointing the way.

Costa Rica looked good. It was odd not to see patrols of soldiers and checkpoints on the way into town. On the surface it seemed as though the troubles of Central America were far, far away and not just simmering on her borders. The downtown was clean and well laid out, with modern buildings and sharply dressed men and women moving briskly.

They pulled up in front of the El Presidente and were met by a bellhop, who took their bags as they checked in. Their guide seemed a bit put out that he had failed to interest them in any of the more cultural sights and events that his country had to offer, and left thinking they were just a couple of more tourists who wanted only to wallow in the sins of the flesh of which his country was nearly as proud as it was of its scenery.

They were taken up to the third floor and shown their room. Clean, a television set, and phone. The bellboy announced proudly that the hotel had hot water most of the time. He knew how Americanos were about hot water; it was almost a fetish with them. The size of the tip disappointed him, but he knew then that they were not first-time tourists to Central America. The tip was generous for a native and incredibly stingy for a green tourist.

They settled in, lying back on their beds. Until

Topo contacted them, there was nothing for them to do but wait. At this stage of the game you never knew what was going to come next. They could pull out in the next five minutes, or have to sit there and have meals brought up to their rooms and spend a week watching the *Million Peso Hombre* on TV. Neither was hungry now; they'd eaten on the flight from Honduras, which had been uneventful but for a bit of uneasiness when they landed at Sandino Airport in Managua.

Getting up, Rossen looked out of the window. In the distance, sitting on top of the ring of mountains surrounding the city, he saw black banks of clouds. It would rain soon. With the evening came the rains. These wouldn't last too long, but with the onset of the rainy season they'd increase.

Braannnng! The coarse ring of another one of Ma Bell's torture instruments startled him out of his weather forecast.

"Hello."

"Señor Rossen?"

"Yeah, this is Rossen." He waited. The voice on the other end wasn't Topo's.

"Señor, we will meet in the morning. Be ready to go on your tour of the countryside."

Rossen grunted back, " *'Sta bien*. We'll be ready."

"*Buenas noches*, then, señores. Enjoy your evening, and *buena suerte*."

Hanging up, Rossen wondered why everyone was always wishing him good luck.

"Okay, Tommy, get your ass off the bed and we'll see what this town has to offer. I could use a beer."

Outside, dark had fallen. Directly across from the hotel was a small lounge, where faces in the window

blended with the lights and shadows. They didn't
stop there, though, it was too close to the hotel.
Going to the corner, they turned and walked a couple
of blocks. They could see a sign that said THE AMSTEL
a block ahead. Rossen knew that just past it was the
Key Largo; he had a friend there, but it was too early
for him to be in. They'd drop by later.

One thing he'd learned about Costa Rica was that
they had more thieves per square foot than anyplace
he'd ever been. Ahead, three men leaned against the
side of a building, smoking and talking. One of them
obviously owned the cab at the curb, and Rossen
recognized the other two as pimps.

From the narrow doorway of a hotel a girl lurched
out drunkenly toward them, promising exotic plea-
sures in her room if they'd just go up the stairs with
her. She made a bad mistake and picked on Tommy
first, using the old game of grabbing a dude by his
balls with one hand while going for his billfold with
the other.

Tomanaga knew the game, too. At the moment her
nimble and sober fingers went for his pocket, his
steel claw went down. She started to scream as Tommy
pushed her back up into the open doorway. She
couldn't move. Tommy's claw was firmly placed and
set between her legs, the pointed end up. She was
balanced on his hook.

"Listen to me, *puta*. Stay away from us." He
eased the pressure, leaving her doubled over, squatting in the doorway, holding her money-maker and
cursing them. The two pimps had started to move,
until Rossen stood between them and grinned. One
put his hand into his pocket as if reaching for some-

thing. Rossen nodded at him agreeably and motioned for him to come on. He didn't.

The pimp made a quick value judgment. These were not his normal prey, and the girl, she was nothing. She was getting too old to make money hooking, and obviously her fingers had gone, too. They could get another who was much better. She was of no importance. The man removed his hand from his pocket and smiled pleasantly, showing his empty hands. Rossen tapped Tommy on the shoulder. "Let's go get that beer. There's nothing here."

They turned to go back down the street. The one who'd stuck his hands in his pocket stepped forward one pace. Mustering up some bravado, he pointed at the larger man and his steel-fingered friend.

"Hasta luego, amigos."

Before he knew it, Rossen had him by his shirt, jerked up, back against a wall, his feet a foot off the ground. There was a hand around his throat, the thumb digging in around the cartilage of his esophagus.

"Not later, son of a bitch. Right now if you want it!"

He let the pimp slide back to the pavement. His friend had made no move. He knew there was a time to keep one's mouth shut. Stepping away, he turned and went across the street, fading into darkness. In the doorway the girl whimpered and swore at them, her hands holding her tender parts gently. Rossen knew from the look in the pimp's eyes that this last demonstration was all that was needed. He'd bother them no more. He was one who was more used to scaring and beating up women and drunks. He had no taste for his own pain.

They went down the street and turned the corner to the left, experiencing a rush. The Club New Yorker was right in front of them. Somehow, it seemed that no matter where in the world they went that there was trouble, they would find a saloon named the New Yorker. They pushed open the swinging doors and stepped inside. A couple of bar girls eyed them speculatively. The club was narrow, just a single row of booths on the right-hand side and a bar on the left, which sat ten to twelve. Behind it was the bartender, who smiled at Rossen, showing one gold tooth in an otherwise perfect set of teeth. She was obviously pregnant.

"Yes, whach chu want, amigo?" She eyed Tommy curiously; there weren't many Orientals here.

Rossen ordered for them. *"Dos cervezas, por favor."*

"Two beers. Es Imperial hokay, chu speak pretty good espanich. Where chu from? New York?"

To Carolina Lopez Feldstein, whose husband was from New York, that was always the first question.

Rossen shook his head. The beer was good, cold, and sharp. Apparently, a lot of good German brewmasters had moved to Central America at one time or another.

Tommy had two of the bar girls flanking him by now. They seemed fascinated by his steel claw and surprised that he spoke English so well. The other customers at the bar were typical: some tourists, a couple of *pensiones* who had moved south to make their retirement plans go a bit further, and the Latins. From the rear booth two men kept their eyes on the two newcomers. Dark men, small but strongly built, they looked all around them with bitter eyes. Rossen noticed their looks and for a brief second he and the one facing him touched and locked eyes. The Latin looked away, turning his gaze back to his companion. Neither of them had a bar girl to sit with, and none of the girls seemed inclined to go and hustle them.

One of the *pensiones*, a man in his middle sixties, still looking tan and fit though his hair had long gone, spoke over the rim of his beer glass to Rossen.

"Don't pay any attention to them. Those sonsabitches don't like nothing, especially Americans."

The old-timer turned so he could face the men in the rear.

"Ola," he yelled at them. They automatically stared at him. He stuck his middle finger up in the air and growled at them. *"Por sus madres!"*

The hate from their eyes cut through the cigarette smoke. Rossen had a sudden feeling of affection for this tough old man.

"What's their problem?"

"Sandinistas. They're with the Nicaraguan embassy, which has connecting garden doors with the Russians. They're pissed 'cause no one here thinks of them as liberators. Besides that, when they *can* get laid, it costs them three times as much. Fucking Commies!"

Rossen knew he liked the old man and stuck out his hand.

"My name's Rossen."

Taking Rossen's hand in a firm, strong grip, the old man said, "O'Brian. Pleased to meet you." Rossen introduced him to Tommy. Their new acquaintance didn't seem surprised by—or even interested in—Tommy's steel hook. Without it being said, Rossen knew the old man had seen his share of war and mutilation, and knew that Rossen had, too. It was strange how one could tell when another man had shared the same experiences.

In their rear booth, the two Sandinistas were fuming with humiliation. To be insulted by swinish, overbearing, and vulgar gringos was nearly more than they could bear. They were entitled to respect; they had kicked the Americans out of Nicaragua, killed the pig Somoza and regained control of the destiny of their country the same as their comrades in socialism had done in Vietnam. The gringos were the losers, not they.

They were men with a destiny who served honorably the interests of their homeland. In addition to which, they had diplomatic immunity as officials with their embassy. The honor of their nation rested with them. Each of them made another mental note to remember O'Brian when they took over Costa Rica. They knew he was supporting the Contras from his farm near Santa Eugenia. Planes landed and took off in the dark of night. The sheds on his finca were used as storage centers for supplies, and wounded were often flown to his farm and from there taken to other places for treatment. He was an enemy, and the Costa Rican government did nothing to stop him. He should have been deported years ago for interfering in the affairs of his host country.

O'Brian took a pull of his beer and laughed. "Those fuckers hate us, but I guess that's not uncommon anymore. Most of the world seems to have a hard-on for us. We should just let them all stew in their own juice for a while, cut off the money and the aid, block all the fuckers off our list for just a year, then watch them turn around."

Tommy ordered a whiskey—the beer was a bit too sharp for his taste. Carolina set them up, watching them carefully. All kinds came in here. These two had a look to them that was a bit different. That they had been soldiers once was obvious. What they were now was harder to answer. Hers was not a large country, and new faces that hung around over ten days were easily noticed. Most of those who did stay were either on the run and looking for a refuge, or they had the bad eyes of violent men who came here looking to hire their guns out. Most of them went away. There was no money in the coffers of the Contras to pay for mercenaries. A few who came stayed and fought for the Contras anyway. For these, the excitement was payment enough.

Carolina wiped a wet ring from the bar. These two were not quite like the others. She would figure it out if they stayed long enough. Carolina Feldstein prided herself on her ability to figure people out. She had always thought she would have made a good psychologist.

O'Brian knew the different types, too. "You guys going to be around long?"

Rossen shook his head. "Just a few days. We're just taking a break for a while, then back to work." He knew the old man was fishing, and it was best to give him something he could believe. There was no way they'd ever be able to convince him that they worked for the Peace Corps.

"Me and Tommy are in the security consultant business. We go into a troubled area and train local security people and guard forces. We've got a few days off before going to the next job in Honduras, and I'd rather spend my time here than in San Pedro Sula.''

O'Brian nodded. The story was plausible enough. They looked right for it. At least they didn't try any of that rich tourist or playboy shit. Security? If they weren't CIA or from one of the other God-knows-how-many so-called intelligence agencies, well, maybe it was true. There were a lot of men left over from the wars wandering around Central and South America doing the same thing. Not as many as there were when he'd first come south. Back then, every time you turned around you'd stumble over a German, Limey, or Yank. Now most of them, like him, had settled into one place, raised their families, and were just waiting to see what was going to happen next.

These new ones, the ones from Vietnam, would be the same. For a time they'd wander around lost, then those that didn't get killed would either go home and pump gas or a few, like him, would find a place they liked and dig in. He wondered if these two men were his replacements.

Someone turned up the stereo and O'Brian growled at Carolina: ''Give me a break, *mi corazón*, turn that shit down.'' He wasn't very fond of ''Michael Jackson.''

9

From a booth two down from the Sandinistas, a voice soft but strangely familiar asked, "Buy you old-timers a drink?"

Turning, Rossen saw a shadow rise up from the booth and come toward him. Tommy recognized him first.

"My God. Sam Benson."

Benson came over and Tommy broke into a big, happy grin. Benson had been with them in 'Nam: He was the one who had flown Rossen into the gunfight with the Cong shooter and then come back for them.

"What the hell are you doing here, Benson?"

"Oh, just kicking around. I've got me another friend of yours here. Top, come on out." From the booth another shadow rose, and kept rising—massive, broad-shouldered, and with a distinct limp.

"Virden? Is that you?" Rossen almost shouted.

Former Master Sergeant Virden came over and joined the group, hugging Tommy and Rossen around the shoulders until bones threatened to give way. "Yeah, it's me."

O'Brian watched all this with a jaundiced Irish eye. Virden winked at him. "It's okay, Irish. You're in good company. They are two very old friends. Okay now, boys, I'm going to buy the next round and then we're going to cut out of here and find a quiet corner so we can play a little catch-up."

Carolina set them up with pleasure. It was obvious that she liked Virden and Benson. They caused no trouble, paid their bills, and were always polite. Nice gringos, not like most of them—middle-aged tourists who came to Costa Rica to recapture a part of their past when they were young and virile and could have beautiful young ladies at no cost.

"What are you doing out here, Sarge? Did you take your retirement?" Rossen asked.

"Yeah, they medicked me out after I got out of the hospital at Womack. When we got hit in the chopper, a three-inch piece of my thigh went out of the door. But they do pretty good work with stainless steel and plastic, so I can get around as long as I don't do any broad jumps or side straddle hops. I always hated to do them anyway, so it's no big loss."

Rossen took another pull of his beer. "What are you up to?"

"Up to? That sounds like I was doing something less than ordinary. No. I'm just a dedicated public servant doing a little double-dipping by working on my second pension. I'm with the U.S. Information Service at the embassy."

"And you, Benson, are you with them also?"

"No, I just do a little contract flying. You know,

machinery here, fertilizer there. That's all, nothing fancy.''

In their booth the two Sandinistas continued to fume, fueling their anger on another bottle of local rum, which made them even more angry, because the gringos were able to afford good scotch whiskey and they had to drink the cheap shit. But the rum was sweet and hot in the guts, giving them a feeling of righteous indignation that had to be expressed. After all, they did have diplomatic immunity.

Lopez Portrillo rose from the booth, face flushed with his passion.

"You gringos! Why don't you go home. You do not belong here, unless you want another Vietnam. Go home while you are still able to. This land is ours and you cannot have it. We are the new masters here. Go home!''

Virden turned to face the smaller Nicaraguan. "Why don't you and your comrade just go back to your embassy. I'm sure there's at least one Russian hanging around there waiting for you to kiss his ass before he fucks you in yours.''

Portrillo could not tolerate the situation any longer. "Fat gringo pig. *Porco desgraciado.*''

Virden looked at Rossen. "God, I'd love to bust this little bastard's head open, but I can't, I'm still working for the government.''

Portrillo drew his hand back, preparing to deliver a righteous and deserved slap to the face of the ugly fat man who had dared impugn his honor.

"Well, I can,'' Rossen said. At the same time his hand flew out in a fist, connecting squarely right in the middle of the Sandinista's face. Cartilage gave way as the nose broke, spewing blood. Portrillo stumbled back on his heels, hurtling to the end of the bar, knocking over glasses and chairs.

His comrade rose to his aid, coming at Rossen from the back, a beer bottle in his hand. He began to scream. Tommy had moved around on his seat. His steel claw firmly imbedded itself in the thin skin between the collarbone and thick muscles of the shoulder. The hook was set two inches into raw tissue.

Rossen didn't have to follow up on Portrillo; Carolina had him. She came at the Sandino from behind the bar, a sawed-off cue stick in her hand. The rest of the drinkers almost felt sorry for him as hollow thunks sounded from his head and back as the angry woman beat the shit out of him, chasing him to the door, her pregnant belly swaying back and forth as she cursed him.

"Chu go back home. Sandino dog. We don't want you in Costa Rica. Go home to your pigsty and your Russians and your Cubans. This is not Nicaragua. Go home and do not come back again." She chased him down the street, swinging her club with an efficacy proven by the cries of pain coming from Portrillo as he sought to outrun the pregnant woman.

Rossen nodded at Tommy, who released his captive and wiped his hook on a bar towel. Portillo's comrade scuttled out of the bar suddenly, much diminished in size and arrogance; fearful, he avoided a swing of Carolina's club and raced after his comrade to the safety of their embassy and their immunity. But they *could* do one thing; they would report to their chief of security the presence of the new gringos— the Oriental and the big one—who were obviously friends of the CIA man, the fat cripple, Virden. They were most certainly enemies of the revolution, and would bear watching.

Carolina returned to her bar accompanied by applause and cheers. Virden gave her a fatherly hug as she passed. "You're a good kid, Carolina, but be careful about what you mix into. You're not in any shape for a lot of track work."

She snapped her fingers above her head haughtily. "Gordito, *mi corazón*, Carolina can take care of herself . . . and chu, too."

O'Brian grunted, pleased. "You know she can, too. That is one little Nica it is best to have as a friend. Well, I know you guys have a lot to catch up on and I've got to get back to the farm and keep an eye on things.

"Mr. Rossen, Tomanaga, gentlemen, it is a pleasure meeting you. If you ever find yourself in need of a place to crash or rest for a few days, Virden can tell you how to reach me. Good night." O'Brian's broad, strong old back disappeared into the dark.

"You know, I like him."

"Me, too, Rossen, but like he said, we have a few things to talk about. Let's go. Sam why don't you and Tommy keep each other company while I talk to the shooter?"

Benson was agreeable. "We'll go across the street to the Casa Blanca and play some blackjack and meet you at the Key Largo in a couple of hours."

Virden looked at Rossen, who agreed. "Sounds good. . . .The Key Largo in two hours."

Virden led the way, taking Rossen down the street a couple of blocks to a coffeehouse where the customers were few. Finding a table near the rear where they could watch the door, Virden ordered for them, waited until they were served, then leaned forward.

"You're going to get your ass into a lot of trouble if you're not careful, Rossen."

Looking over Virden's shoulder at the people passing by on the other side of the window, Rossen said, "You're a spook now, aren't you, buddy?"

"You know I can't answer that."

"You don't have to. We both been around too much not to know the game. You know about as much about USIS as I do. So let's just cut the bullshit to the minimum."

Virden sighed heavily, and rubbed his right thigh. "Okay, let's just say I'm in a position to know things, and one of the things I knew was that you and Tommy were coming this way. And if I know, so do a lot of other people. And not all of them are as fond of you as I am.

"Now, what are you doing down here?"

"If you know as much as you say, then you should know it's a simple training job for a few weeks, then we're gone."

Virden shook his head. "Wish I could buy that, but we both know what it is you do best and that's shoot—not teach. You have a target?"

"No, I don't. The job is just what I said, and if you knew I was coming, you also know who the contractors are. So you can stop me or leave me alone . . . which is it going to be?"

Virden rose to pay the tab. "You're on your own. But the word is there's a hit in the making and it has our friends to the north a bit upset. We don't want waves in Costa Rica. So be cool here, or something ugly may happen to you and I really wouldn't like that. I owe you too much. Just remember how the game is played: friends today, dead tomorrow. If you decide you want to talk to me, you can reach me at the embassy; they'll contact me anytime of the day or night.''

Leaving the café, they headed back up the street.

"Rossen, I want you to know that personally I don't give a shit if you waste every fucking Sandino in Nicaragua. Just don't do anything here. This is my turf, and I'm responsible. All I have to do is say the word and you'll be kicked out of the country within the hour. Now, let's forget it for a while and go see how Benson and Tommy are getting on.''

At the corner, Rossen saw the hooker who had tried to pick Tomanaga's pocket. Her pimps were still there, and when they saw Rossen, they scurried like rats back into the safety of the shadows on the stairway.

Virden watched them. "You know Sucking Sue, I see. Doesn't look to me like you're one of her favorite people.''

Grinning in the dark, Rossen laughed. "Not me. Let's just say she got herself hoisted on Tommy's fishing hook when she went too deep in his pocket.''

Virden laughed. "You mean?''

"Yeah, she got a free and almost instantaneous hysterectomy.'' They reached the entrance to the Key Largo, once a beautiful colonial-type house that was getting a bit rundown but still was filled with life. The life of Costa Rica.

10

Virden led the way into the club. It had the feel of the tropics to it, not what you'd expect to find in native bars on the coast, but in one that was a blend of the old world and the West Indies. James, the owner, came up to greet Virden. "Hey, Sarge, how's it going?"

"Pretty well, Chinaman. I'd like you to meet a friend of mine, Jim Rossen. We were in 'Nam together a thousand or two years ago."

They shook hands and James told them that Tomanaga and Sam Benson were out back. They joined them and settled in. Virden ordered a whiskey and Rossen a bourbon and dish of ceviche to go with it.

"Did you call him Chinaman?" Rossen asked the sergeant.

Virden smiled. "Yeah, it's kind of a private joke. James has an Oriental look to his eyes and not too long ago he came down with a bad case of hepatitis, turned the prettiest yellow you ever saw." Nodding his head at Tomanaga, he said, "No offense of course, Tomanaga."

"None taken, Sarge. It happens to be one of my favorite colors. Did you and Rossen have a good talk?"

"Yeah, we understand each other. How did you guys do at the blackjack table?"

Benson looked sulky. "I dropped about a hundred and it's in Tommy's pocket."

Tomanaga called for a waiter to order a round. "Then don't feel too bad. You'll get part of it back. Internally."

"Not too much; we'll have to go pretty soon," Rossen said.

Tomanaga knew what he meant. They'd drawn too much attention to themselves already.

"Okay, boss, we'll go whenever you're ready. I'm tired anyway. Guess I'm getting old. Can't take the hours and travel anymore."

The next hour was spent watching the crowd. The whores that came in took up positions at strategic places in the club. They were well-mannered, well-dressed, and didn't hit on any of the customers. If you wanted to talk to them, you had to go to them. House rules, it seemed.

The people at the bar were mostly tourists mixed in with a few obvious regulars who ignored the girls and listened to the calypso duo singing in the rear.

Virden was obviously at home. He pointed out different characters. "That one is a dope dealer from Colombia who comes here four or five times a year for vacation. There's a couple of *pensiones* who have small farms up in the mountains, and those nice, clean-cut-looking young men over by the shuffleboard are Los Angeles pot dealers. They don't buy it here; they have farms in California. They'll be leaving soon, it's about time to get their seedlings started. You'll find a lot of different types here, but one thing goes for everybody at the Key Largo. Behave yourself.''

Leaning over conspiratorially, Virden added, ''Every now and then we even get some ex-soldier-types looking for work or thrills. They usually don't hang around too long. There's not much here for them. All the action is pretty well kept under control . . . if you know what I mean.''

Rossen took that as his cue to get his hat and get gone. ''I know what you mean, Sarge. And it's time for me and Tomanaga to turn in. We might have a busy day tomorrow. If not, maybe we'll catch you later.''

''You do that, shooter. You keep in touch with me for both our sakes.''

They passed the pickpocket and her wounded pussy. Tomanaga bowed to her and scratched his own crotch with his hook and grinned evilly, aiming a come-to-me gesture with the shiny steel hook. Her pimps glowered and looked away. They'd be glad when these two were gone and they could go back to normal hunting.

Once they were back in their room, Tomanaga stripped down and hit the sack, groaning at the sheer pleasure of clean cool sheets against his skin.

''You know that Virden's a spook now, don't you?''

Rossen turned off the lights and crawled into bed. "Yeah, I know, but he's still all right. He's trying to get along, that's all. What about Sam?"

Tomanaga turned to his side, and took off his claw, rubbing the stump with his good hand. "He's just what he said he was, though I'm sure he does a little work for the Company now and then. He's got an old gooney bird that he hauls some cargo in, or he'll fly some other dude's bird on charter. He's tight with Virden, but I don't think he's in bed with him all the way or he wouldn't have talked so freely, even if we were pretty tight back in the old days."

"Yeah, you're probably right. Did you get a number? We might need him sometime. It's always good to know someone who can fly, especially if he has his own plane." Rossen was asleep before Tommy could answer.

Virden left the Key Largo, stopping at the Nashville South a block away for a beer before returning to the embassy. He liked the Nashville South: It wasn't as hectic as the Key Largo, and the music—though he wasn't a country-music buff—reminded him of home. Jack and Duff, the owners, were both there. They'd come south years ago, liked it, stayed, married, and wouldn't have been at ease Stateside anymore.

"*Hola*, Virden, how's it going?"

"Okay, Duff. You and Jack keeping the natives busy?"

Duff grinned, looking more Italian than Irish. "Yeah, we gotta stay on their ass all the time."

A couple of shoeshine boys stuck their heads in to see if there was any business to be had. Virden, like most of the natives, had taken to wearing sneakers to keep from being hounded by the hordes of shoeshine boys that worked the streets. One shine a day is all right, but after being hit on ten to fifteen times in a couple of hours, one had to take preventive measures.

Leaving Jim and Duff to the twangy howlings of some country bumpkin, Virden went on to the embassy, checked at the desk for messages, and headed for his office on the second floor. From his window he could see the Marine sentries patrolling the grounds. Embassies had been pretty hard hit in the last couple of years.

Unlocking a file cabinet, he removed a folder. In it were the life and times of one Jim Rossen and his partner. He knew the past intimately; he'd been part of it. It was the present that concerned him. Rossen was here to make a hit. The prospect of him killing more people wasn't anything new. When Rossen was around, insurance salesmen took a loss.

Maybe he really didn't know what the Contras had in mind for him. Topo was a pretty shrewd character. It was true that Rossen had never in the past worked as a hired assassin. True, he had snuffed a few "selected targets" in Southeast Asia, but that had been for our side and he had still been in the service. Had he changed? Virden reached farther back in the cabinet, taking out a well-used liter of Johnnie Walker Black. He poured a not too generous portion into a water glass and sat down.

The problem was that Costa Rica wanted to stay

out of it, and the State Department was very touchy about American mercenaries creating problems. If Rossen and Tomanaga were doing just as they'd said—going in to run some training classes—the embassy would be glad to turn a blind eye. But if they were killed, or taken prisoner by the Sandinistas, then that was a whole different bag of shit.

He'd have his man in the *comandante*'s HQ try to find out more. Until then he'd just try to keep them out of trouble. If he had to, he'd see they were deported for their own protection.

As far as he was concerned, if what he had heard was true and they were coming in to off Colonel Sergie Rasnovitch and his ass-kisser Luis Guzman, he wished them luck. It was about time those two cocksuckers got a taste of their medicine.

Virden wasn't a man often given to deep philosophical thought, but sometimes he wondered if maybe terrorism wouldn't end up being the salvation of the civilized world. Peace and reason might become the rule of the day among the world leaders when they realized that they—the presidents, premiers, and brains—were on the front line, that they were going to be hit before the poor GI was. When their own precious asses were placed in firm and sure jeopardy, they just might come to understand that that would leave the rest of the world the fuck alone.

Tired, he finished the last of the scotch and put the bottle and the file away. Tomorrow was another day, and maybe he'd have some good news, like Congress getting off its collective social conscience and sending the Contras some money and supplies. They were hanging on by a pubic hair now. He didn't doubt that

the politicians would eventually get their shit together, but every day they waited cost lives. Minutes
were paid for in blood. Stupid shits! They should get
off their office asses and get into the real world
they've created for the rest of us to live in.

*I'd rather have a sister in a whorehouse than
a son in politics. At least she'd be doing something to earn her money.* Disgusted, he locked up.
It was late, he was late, the whole fucking world was
late, and there wasn't a damned thing he could do
about it.

There were others who were working late in offices on Dzherinsky Square in Moscow to Havana,
Washington to Tegucigalpa. Men punched buttons
and data came forth. Names, dates, places. Profiles
and contingency plans. Nothing ever really came to a
halt; there were only shift changes, but the machines
worked around the clock. In one office, banks of
computers were searching and cross-referencing a
request for information on a man called Rossen, or
shooter, who had a one-handed Japanese associate.
Through the marvels of electronics and satellite communications, the request was being researched within
three hours of the office in Managua receiving it.

Dawn came at the same time as the phone call.
This time Rossen knew the voice. Juliano.
"Are you ready, señor?"
"Yeah. Where do we meet?"
"I am downstairs at this moment. Please come

now. Bring nothing with you, your bags will be picked up later and brought to you."

"Okay, we'll be down in five minutes."

Christ, they didn't believe in giving a guy much warning. But it's their dime.

"Roll out, Tommy, we gotta go. Juliano is downstairs saying come as we are."

Tomanaga was already wide awake, and by the time five minutes had elapsed, they were exiting the elevator in the lobby. Juliano came to them. Rossen eyed the desk clerk. Juliano followed his look.

"Don't worry, amigos, he is one of us. Let us go. Things are progressing rapidly, and I believe that you attracted a bit too much attention last night. It will be best to get you out of town."

Rossen regretted not being able to spend a day or two more in San José. The town looked and felt good: nice people, pretty women, good food, great climate.

Juliano led them out to a ten-year-old Ford pickup and took them through a number of side roads around the town, keeping an eye on his rearview mirror to see if they were followed.

At last satisfied that they didn't have anyone on their tail, Juliano headed up a long driveway through a heavy metal gate with two guards on it. Rossen had spotted several other men in the trees and brush alongside the driveway leading up to the gate. The HQ was a large two-story mansion left over from better days. Around the house were a great number of young, healthy men with the sincere look in their eyes of those fighting a holy war.

Inside, they were taken past Topo's secretary.

Rosalia turned it on, giving Rossen a sensuous brown-
eyed appraisal as only Latin women can, laying a
look of curiosity on Tommy and his claw. She liked
what she saw and what she knew of them. The gringo
was the shooter, the one who would kill the Russian
and Guzman for the *comandante*. That automatically qualified him for some clandestine movements
of her own.

Going up the stairs, Rossen was aware of Rosalia.
He had the same feeling between his shoulder blades
that you get when you know you're in someone's
telescopic sight, the trigger slack being taken up.

Topo rose to welcome them.

"Please, sit.

"You were busy last night. But I am glad to know
that you are friends of Señor Virden's. He is a good
man and does what he can for us. And the pilot,
Benson, he has done some work for us in the past. I
tell you this to make you feel more secure as to our
intentions. As for the two Communists you had problems with, they are of no real importance. But to be
on the safe side, I think it is best if we send you up to
the zone today."

There wasn't much to be said. Rossen and Tommy
knew Topo was right. "Okay. We're ready to go
anytime. How do we travel?"

"You will be driven up. We are sending up a
couple of men and some supplies. I will probably be
up to talk with you in a few days. That will give you
time to look around and get the feel of things and
meet our people. Juliano will be there sooner.

"So, your bags should already be loaded and you
can leave after you have lunch. I hope you enjoy it.

Our daily fare on the zone does not have much variety to it.''

Juliano led them outside after lunch to their transport.

"I will see you soon. I would ride up with you, but I have a flight to make tonight. Have a good trip, and *buena suerte*."

11

They loaded up in a faded red and white Land-Rover for the ride to the frontier. Rossen was given the front passenger seat as a sign of his importance, while the other two passengers and Tomanaga were stuffed in the back as comfortably as possible among the gear they were taking up. The two Contras smiled happily, in good spirits. One of them, a thin curly-headed black with a Nikon hung on a strap around his neck, nodded happily at them. He was going up to the front to take pictures for their propaganda department. The other was a Miskito Indian just released from the hospital, where he'd had some pieces of shrapnel removed. He was glad to be going back, too. His wife and children were still in the jungle waiting for him. Both men accepted the presence of the Americans easily. Manuel Torres, the photographer, had to resist temptation. Picture-taking was his job and his passion. But he had been told quite clearly: no pictures of the gringos and no questions about why they were going to the zone. He had been told they were shooting instructors and that was all. He'd ask nothing else. Topo always meant what he said, and Manuel had no desire to join the unknown destinations of several others who had found out about Topo's sincerity the hard way. He'd ask nothing and hear less.

At the airport junction they took the road to the left leading up into the hills. It was going to be a four-hour ride to Petel, where the blacktop ended, then another three or four on dirt roads. Rossen wasn't pleased that the rains were starting, and the rattle of the windshield wipers and jolting of the Land-Rover on the rutted road made it hard to catch any sleep—his preferred way to travel. They passed through a number of small towns, more modern-looking than those they'd seen in Guatemala or Honduras, more gringo than Spanish. As they went over a ridge of mountains the driver pointed out a bend in the road where there had been an attempt on the life of the *comandante*. Then they began to drop down, heading back to sea level. Rossen knew that from now on the days and nights would be much warmer. Why couldn't anyone ever have a war where the countryside and climate was pleasant. *No!* The sonsabitches always had to pick the most miserable climates to fight in, snow or jungle, swamps and deserts. . . .

They stopped once for chow. Rossen was surprised at the driver's lack of concern for their security, and also by the same lack of interest in the eyes of the Costa Ricans they passed on the way. Maybe they had just learned to mind their own business and ignore the comings and goings of the Contras, for he was sure the vehicle was recognized even if the driver wasn't. They ate at Petel, near the end of the blacktop, and when the blacktop ended, so did the electricity. Their meal was a bland-tasting mixture of some kind of stewed chicken and rice with the ever-present black beans as a side dish.

Just after dark they stopped at a Costa Rican checkpoint. Two young guards with 5.56mm Galil assault rifles stood their post, a makeshift hut of reeds and canvas. The driver whispered to Rossen, "No talking. They have a radio, and the transmitter is always left on so their HQ can listen in."

The guards knew who they were, but went through the charade of questions and answers. The gringo and his friend the Oriental had been identified as a couple of *periodistas,* journalists, going up to the zone for a look-see. The guards knew they were lying, flashed their lights on Rossen's face, then on Tomanaga's, cast the beam around over the boxes of equipment. One of them looked Rossen right in the eye, made a thumbs-up sign and smiled, whispered to them, and motioned them on. The shooter liked that. If the Guardia was on the side of the Contras, at least in spirit, it was a good sign. The Costa Ricans didn't like the idea of having a Cuba on their border, and if the Contras could kick them out, then *buena suerte*— good luck, that's what the sentry had whispered as he waved them on.

Rossen had no idea of where they were. The road twisted and turned over slippery red clay tracks broken by flashes of lightning and accented by the dull roar of thunder rolling over the black hills and valleys. It was nearly 2000 hours when the Land-Rover came to a stop. In its headlights he saw a two-story unpainted clapboard structure in front of them.

Groaning, knees stiff and bladders full, they unassed their conveyance and stretched their legs. Their driver whistled once, then again. A shadow detached itself from the side of the building. A man of around sixty with a distinguished white-gray beard, wearing a Johnson Outboard Motors baseball cap, short-sleeve khaki shirt, and a Bulgarian AK-47 greeted them.

The driver made introductions.

May I present Don Jorge. This is his house we will stay at for the night. He has the job of keeping the motors in good repair for the pongas, the canoes, and boats. Rossen sniffed the air. He could smell the river over the fresher taste of the rain, but he couldn't see it.

Don Jorge greeted them with a simple: *"Bienvenidos a la zona."*

"Yeah, welcome to the zone." Rossen'd heard that before. Don Jorge led them into his house. The floor was dirt. In the corner was an old Westinghouse refrigerator that didn't work but was handy for keeping things in. On one wall was a poster of the *comandante* in full uniform sitting in the back of a vehicle and looking very correct and courageous. The poster translated into something about: First we had the oppression of the Somozas, now we have the tyranny of the Communists. I say, no more tyrants. Fight—or live as slaves. . . .

He'd seen signs like that before, too. Once they had their gear inside, they ate by the light of a kerosene lamp. Again the meal consisted of black beans and rice, but with something new added. From the refrigerator Jorge removed a few cans of tuna and sardines. The fridge was stuffed with cans and nothing else. The driver looked at them and shrugged.

"Canned fish is cheap here, and it is nourishing. You will get used to it." Rossen wasn't sure he wanted to, but Tomanaga just smacked his lips and dug into a couple of tins before settling down for the night.

He and Tomanaga found posts that held the second floor up and tied their jungle hammocks to them, then maneuvered their bodies into them. They had started to settle down when Jorge went outside and came back with two AK-47s and placed one by each man's hammock. Don Jorge spit through his gray beard, motioned up the stairs, mumbled something about *"Mi esposa,"* and left them.

Tommy looked over at Rossen. Both men took the weapons and checked them over. They weren't the cleanest they'd ever seen, but they would work, and each had a full magazine. They felt better. The giving of weapons removed the uneasy feeling they had carried with them all the way from San José. They had their security blankets.

The flame on the lamp was extinguished. The night was heavily dark, the rain still falling but beginning to lighten up a bit. In the distance they heard a hacking whoop. Monkeys.

Each tried to get as comfortable as he could in the fishnet jungle hammocks, and neither one took off his boots. Their driver had gone upstairs with their host. In a flash of lightning Rossen saw eyes watching him from the hard-packed earthen floor. A huge frog or toad. He never could tell which. It cocked its head, reached out its tongue, and whipped into its gaping maw an inch-long beetle, then hopped slowly, confidently, closer to its gritty-eyed observer's hammock, where it was joined by two slightly smaller relatives.

"Listen, fellows, you keep the mosquitos off me and I won't stomp on you."

The boss frog swelled out his throat as if to say, *Okay, gringo, we got a deal. You go on to sleep and we'll keep watch.*

Rossen slept lightly, unused to the hammock. It would take a while to be comfortable in one again. Twice he woke, got up, and went outside, taking the Russian-made assault rifle with him. Once just to listen, to feel the aura, get the taste of the place. It, too, was familiar, the night heavy. One of Jorges' farm dogs came and sat down beside him. He found a large tree stump to hang his legs over. The dog, like all hound dogs, seemed content to sit by the stranger and have his ears occasionally scratched by the newcomer. It was near dawn. Standing up, Rossen stretched his arms and rocked back and forth on his heels to loosen the muscles in his legs. The ground was spongy under his feet. While he was up he unzipped his fly and pissed against the stump, then leaned over it, trying to sort things out in his mind and forecast what the next days would bring. The *comandante* did not have a reputation for liking gringos. And after the way he had been fucked around by them, Rossen didn't blame him much. During their journey the driver hadn't said much of anything. Maybe he'd been given orders not to. If so, that would be the first real attempt at any security he'd seen so far. Everyone seemed to be pretty casual about the situation. He'd expected to pass checkpoints along the way, especially this close to the frontier.

Dawn would be on them soon. It got light at about six in this region of the tropics. He liked it this way. It was the quiet time.

He looked through the dark to where the river was. Listening closely, he could hear it, the gurgling of the hidden waters running to the sea. In the distance, he couldn't tell how far, he saw the glow of a campfire and knew that it came from the Nicaraguan side of the border. Indian country. . . . "Charley land."

He thought he heard the cry of a baby, then it was gone, leaving only fading night. The pre-dawn came, and with the false light everything around him looked as though it belonged in a spook show, with wavering outlines of coco palms, trees, and bushes. A rooster crowed once, then again, and was joined from across the river by another. The haze lightened. He breathed deeply. The land was rich with odors and new smells and some not so new. Wood smoke drifted from across the river to him. Now he could barely make out the shape of a couple of huts looking as though they were floating on a cloud. Thin wisps rose from them, thicker and darker. Inside the huts, he knew, the women would be getting ready to rise and fix food for their men and children, to gather water from the river and wait for their men to rise and eat.

"Rossen," Tomanaga called from the farmhouse, "Come on in. They're getting chow ready, then Jorge says we're to move out as soon as it's light enough to navigate on the river."

"Yeah, okay, Tomanaga, I'm coming." He patted the hound on its bony head and walked back to the farmhouse.

12

Breakfast consisted of the same thing they'd consumed last night—black beans and rice. Life was frugal on the frontier. Don Jorge's wife came down to fix the meal, a silent woman who smiled pleasantly but looked at her husband as if he were a slightly simple child whom she indulged in his fantasies. Don Jorge wasn't a Nica, he was a Costa Rican and didn't have to be involved—but he was, wholeheartedly. He received no money for his efforts or hospitality; all he wanted was to be part of something bigger than he was, and this was the chance. All of his life he had been a dreamer. His wife claimed that that came of his going to school and learning to read all those silly books about other people and places, when he should have been clearing land for his family to eat and prosper on. But all men are little more than very large children. The biggest problem with them is that their games become too violent and are not restricted to just those who wish to play at heroes and noble causes.

For her there was no cause other than that of rearing their children. To do her best to take care of her man and be laid beside him when they died, where she would spend eternity with him in the arms of all-loving and gentle Jesus. With those objectives her needs and goals were easy. She demanded nothing and gave all.

Rossen and Tommy ate outside, wanting to get a look at the country in the daylight hours. The two guerrillas who had come up with them ate with Don Jorge and his wife. Their driver was already gone. He'd taken off at first light for the long drive back to San José and decent food, women, and whiskey.

"*Hola*, gringos!" Don Jorge pointed to the river. "*Vámonos*."

Grabbing their packs and weapons, they followed him down to the riverbank, where a shack served as a mechanic's shop. Several outboards were in the process of being repaired, and there were pongas and a mixed bag of other boats, including skiffs, and a twenty-foot cabin cruiser waiting Don Jorge's attention. Two men were already there working. They were introduced to Alfredo, Don Jorge's eldest. He'd worked on a Danish luxury liner as a steward for several years before coming home, and his English was better than Rossen's Spanish.

From across the river, where Rossen had seen the fires of the huts during the night, a small ponga with three men in it paddled across the reddish waters to where the motorized boats were tied up. Alfredo hoisted a gunny sack of supplies over his shoulder and motioned for Rossen and Tommy to follow him down to the bank and get on one of the pongas. Behind them came the other two Contras. The log canoes were unstable, and it took some quick footwork until they found their balance and sat down in the bottom of the canoe.

After an awkward spell of shuffling around, everyone got placed so the canoe was reasonably balanced. A pull on the cord of the outboard, and Alfredo gave a smile of contentment as it coughed into life. A couple of adjustments to fine-tune it, and he was satisfied. From the bank Don Jorge waved a farewell and yelled to them, *"Buena suerte, amigos!"*

Rossen cursed under his breath; there it was again. Tomanaga grinned, cradled his AK on his knees, and settled back against the side of the ponga to practice being inscrutable for a while. The day was good: The sun was up, the temperature mild, a slight breeze blowing in from the sea. It was a nice day for a boat ride. Not knowing where they were going didn't seem to bother them much. Alfredo swung the bow of the ponga out, heading into midstream and downriver.

"Hey, Señor Rossen? What are you doing here? You a CIA man?"

Rossen grunted as he tried to adjust to the cold wet spot on his butt. "I'm minding my own business, that's what I'm doing."

Alfredo laughed at him. "No need to get touchy, man. We are all friends here." He paused for a second. "Well, at least most of us are."

Rossen watched the banks of the river: He didn't like it; there were too many places suitable for ambush. Alfredo followed his eyes.

"No need to worry right now, gringo. This area is

fairly secure. The Sandinistas don't like getting in this deep. The only time they hit us this far back, it was with planes. So if you hear plane motors, get ready to swim."

The rough bow of the ponga cut through the murky waters for another hour and a half. It was obvious the river was a critical and major artery for the ARDE people, and they appeared to be in total control of it—or at least this part of it. Pongas filled with guerrillas passed them heading upstream. No one seemed particularly worried about the Sandinistas setting up an ambush or meeting enemy troops on their boats. Rossen relaxed a little, but not as much as Tommy had.

Looking to the front, Rossen could make out a broad patch of beach on the riverbank. Near the bush line, a couple of hundred meters back from the riverbank, were what appeared to be several large huts covered with something black. The ponga pulled into the sandy bank. From the huts several men were coming to meet them. Alfredo stood up and waved, saying something in Spanish too fast for Rossen to follow.

"You, too, gringo. This is where you get off. It's as far as I go. Someone else will take care of you from here on. But if you get back around the farm, stop and say hello. There'll always be a plate of beans and rice."

Grabbing their gear, Rossen and Tommy once more tried to keep their balance and get out of the ponga with a modicum of grace. They failed.

Finally setting their feet on the beach, they hoisted their gear onto their shoulders and waited . . . waited for someone to tell them where to go or what to do.

The men who had come from the huts loaded up the supplies from the ponga and headed back to the black-covered shacks which Rossen now saw were nothing more than bamboo frames covered by huge sheets of plastic.

"Hello, Señor Rossen and Señor Tomanaga. I hope I said your name right," he said to Tommy. "Welcome to the zone. I am Jesus, the *comandante de logistica,* or, as you would say, the supply officer, for this trip. If you will come with me, please, I have someone who has been waiting for you. He would have come out to meet you, but he is busy right now."

Tommy nodded at Rossen as though to say, *Well, now we're getting somewhere*, then said, "Right, you are *comandante*. Lead on; we'll be right behind you." Following after Jesus, they crossed the strip, noticing the sandbagged holes dotting the sides. Firing pits. Rossen's eyes took in the length of the sand landing strip, and recognized the indentations he saw laid out in a regular pattern: There had been a rocket attack here, and not long ago, or the rains would have washed away the signs. The beach was mostly gravel, and already turning as hard as concrete from the increasing heat of the morning. By midday it would be near a hundred, with matching humidity.

Nearing the black-topped huts, Rossen could see the men in them. Most were lying around on hammocks stretched out between poles, while others were sorting through packs, separating them. In the rear of one of the huts he could see the back of a man kneeling on the floor. There was something about the body, the way the man moved, that struck a chord. Familiar, but . . .

The man turned around and looked at him.

"Well, you son of a bitch, are you going to stand out there and get sunstroke or give me the fucking package that Juliano gave you for me. I need it now."

Rossen and Tommy froze, looked at each other, then shook their heads.

Chuck DeCarlo, former SF medic and general pain in the ass, stood up. His hair had thinned out, but other than that he was the same. Tall, thin, with an ever-present hungry look to his face that Machiavelli would have loved.

"Get moving, you two murdering cocksuckers. I need that shit now!"

Rossen dropped his pack and opened it, taking out the packages that had been given to him in San José. Eagerly, DeCarlo snatched it from his hands and tore at the wrappings.

"Thank God you finally got here." Looking past him, they could see what Chuck had been bent over: a little girl, maybe five or six years old, with brown eyes the size of saucers. Her right arm and thin chest were swathed in bandages. Chuck left them and turned back to her, speaking gently, the tones of caring and concern overlaying every word as he rattled on in quick, fluent Spanish, calling the little Indian child his *corazón,* his *cara,* his sweetheart, and loved one. From the pack he took out a small bottle and quickly filled a syringe from it, swabbed the little girl's thin legs with a cotton ball, and told her he knew she had a brave heart and the hurt wouldn't last long. Dark eyes filled with tears as she bit her lips when the needle entered her thigh. Chuck had always been that way: He didn't care about what adults did to each other, but injured children made him angry, mad, indignant, and, in some cases, violent, when he could get his hands on any part of the anatomy of anyone who had hurt a child.

Kissing the little girl, he picked her up, put her gently into a hammock, and placed a wet cloth on her forehead before turning back to Rossen and Tommy.

Rinsing his hands in a bucket of river water, he gave a half grin to the new arrivals.

"Sorry to be abrupt, but I was busy. Look at that, will you. Some son of a bitch shot her! Can you believe that? Some no-good, motherless son of a piece of slime put three bullets in that baby. God! When I see that, I just want to rip some motherfucker's head off his stinking shoulders and shove it up his ass."

Tommy nodded; Chuck hadn't changed a bit. It was a well-known secret that he had killed two Americans in Vietnam when they'd gotten drunk and tossed a grenade into a Vietnamese family's hooch and killed three children. Chuck had shot them both. Children were his passion.

Rossen moved up to him. "Okay, Chuck, settle down and tell us you're glad to see us, then tell us what the hell you're doing here. Last I heard you were in West Africa."

DeCarlo wiped his now partially clean hands over his face. "What d'ya mean, why am I here? I'm working on my book."

They'd forgotten about that; he had been writing a book for the last twenty years, but no one had ever seen a single page of it.

"Well, that's good. How's it going?"

"Great, just great. After this war is over and I get

back to civilization—if there is such a place—I'll
have a guaranteed best seller. You know, being the
only gringo north of the San Juan, life in the jungle
with the Contras, and all that.'' He eyed Tommy and
Rossen strangely.

"Well, at least I used to be the only gringo north
of the San Juan." Then, bobbing his head at Tommy,
DeCarlo added, "I don't know if you qualify as a
gringo or not. I'll ask the *comandante* next time I
see him."

They moved back under the shade of the plastic
tarp. The heat was getting heavy. Sweat began to
bead and run down their foreheads.

"How's the little girl?" Rossen pointed at her and
gave a thin smile. He'd never been at ease with
children.

Chuck followed his glance and smiled gently, saying
with satisfaction, "She's going to be all right. A
Maule's flying in today for a supply drop in the
mountain where the *comandante*'s at. When it comes
back, it'll put down, and we'll get her out to one of
the children's hospitals in Costa Rica. They take
good care of the kids we can get out. . . . Yeah,
she'll be okay, but there's lots more"—he nodded
toward the jungle—"lots more out there that won't
be."

Jesus stayed close but not too close, listening un-
obtrusively. It was always wise to know as much as
possible. Topo had told him to keep an eye on their
two guests and make certain that nothing happened to
them. They were his responsibility until they left the
LZ. He was glad that other gringo, the medico, was
there. Most of his men also liked him, but too many
still associated all Americans with the Somozas.

The little girl whimpered and called out, "Papa Gringo!"

Chuck left them immediately and went to her. Comforting her, he shook a couple of pills out of a plastic bottle and gave them to her. One thing hadn't changed. Chuck was still being called Papa. Rossen knew he'd been called that in a dozen or more languages. Maybe that was it. Chuck actually believed he was the father of every child in the world.

They left the medic with the child—he'd forgotten they were there. Shouldering their weapons, they went to see if Jesus knew anything about what the plans were for them.

"What now?"

Jesus shrugged as only Latins can. "We wait. . . ."

"For what?"

"Till someone tells me where they want you to go."

"When will that be?"

"Yo no sé."

"Well, if you don't know, who does?"

Jesus wiped his forehead with a piece of cloth cut from a cargo chute. "Be patient, amigos. This is not the American army with all of your marvelous equipment. We have very little here and right now all of it is in use. There is a battle going on near the mountain. When that is over, then you'll be taken inside to see the *comandante*. Till then you are to wait. Maybe one day, maybe five. It depends. But you will go in and maybe"—he paused—"you will wish then that you were back here with me. In there, in the jungle, it is not so good as here."

The day settled into the familiar pattern of wait and then wait some more. It was the same for soldiers all over the world: Hurry up and wait. During the day several bands of guerrillas came by to pick up supplies. Twice they heard the drone of aircraft engines, and had started to head for the brush and cover the first time, recalling Alfredo's warning about planes, but their nervous jump ended almost before it began when they saw that none of the other Contras showed any interest in the engine sounds. Jesus wiped his face, as he seemed to do almost constantly, and told them, "Those are regular flights from Managua to San José. They come over every day at this time. We know to within a few minutes of when they will pass overhead. There will be another"—he looked at his watch—"in one hour and fifteen minutes that will be the last flight for the day. So if you hear anything between now and then or after that, then would be the time to look for shelter."

Rossen went back to the hot shade of the huts and sat down, his back against a pile of small cargo chutes. The day was definitely getting warmer, the air growing heavier with each breath. Small swarms of tiny black flies would appear for a few minutes, then be gone, leaving itchy red spots to mark where they had stopped.

They waited. . . .

DeCarlo passed them, still grumbling, as he came back from a pond to the rear of the huts with a pan full of water. It was time to give his little girl a cooling bath. He mumbled, "Gotta keep her temperature down," and went on.

The sitting and sweating became boring. Rossen and Tommy decided to look around and see where things were located for future reference. To the rear of the huts, on a small rise under the protective canopy of the trees, was the supply depot. The men there looked at the newcomers with curious eyes and hesitant, unsure smiles. They were leery of those they did not know, but Papa Gringo knew them. It was obvious from the manner in which he had spoken to them. From the insulting tones he had used when speaking to the two new gringos, it was clear they had been friends. It was when Papa Gringo didn't like you that the insults stopped. Among several of them it was becoming a matter of pride to be insulted by the skinny medico. He knew more curses than anyone they had ever met.

The camp was small, looking more like a rest stop for a group of deer hunters. Except for the weapons. It was an interesting mixture: M-14s, AK-47s and a couple of Russian light machine-guns. Around the main camp area, Rossen could make out the shapes of several other huts and shelters spread out in the brush.

Perimeter security didn't exist. Discipline was slack. In the center of the camp was a small cleared area, still under the cover of the trees, where chow was cooked and a fallen log served as a bench. He rested his butt on it while Tomanaga went to see what they'd be eating.

"Hey, Rossen, guess what? We're in luck. Today we don't have to eat beans and rice."

"Yeah, what have they got?"

Tommy chortled. "Rice and beans."

Rossen grumbled something about a smart-ass Jap, and went back to his inspection of the camp. Of the half-dozen men lounging about, only two were different, and that was in only two things. First, their weapons were clean. Second, they were older. Most of the Contras he'd seen were young. From about sixteen to early twenties. These two were in their late forties or early fifties. One had an AK, the other an M-14. Rossen motioned for the one with the M-14 to come over. Roberto Melendez rose and came slowly, his rifle sloped over his shoulder.

Rossen pointed to it. *"Con permiso?"* Roberto looked around him. Rossen could tell he was reluctant to let others handle his weapon. A good sign. Perhaps because he thought it would be impolite, or because he didn't know who or what Rossen and his friend were, he handed over his rifle.

Quickly, with the hands of one who has done it ten thousand times, Rossen examined the weapon. It was clean. No signs of rust, the action worked smoothly enough, the bore wasn't pitted, and it had a thin film of oil on the metal parts. Just enough to keep the rust away. Rising from the log, Rossen looked Melendez straight in the eye and handed him back his rifle as he would have if he'd been on parade.

"Excelente, soldado, muy profesional." Roberto's chest swelled with pride. This man, it was clear, was an expert, an aficionado who appreciated the care that one should give to that which his life depended on.

Regaining his weapon, Roberto came to present arms and grinned widely.

"Gracias, señor." He paused. Rossen gave him what he was waiting for.

"Rossen, *yo se amo*, Rossen." Roberto slung his rifle on his shoulder and put out his hand, the hand of a man who had worked the fields all of his life, with calluses that only fifty years of swinging a machete could put on the palms and fingers.

"*Con mucho gusto, Don Rossen, bienvenido a la zona.*"

Bienvenido a la zona.

13

Tommy kept to the rear, an eagle eye on the other Contras, trying to read their reactions to Rossen and his actions. They didn't seem to be very surprised to see him. In fact, he had noticed more odd looks coming his way than Rossen's, but he was getting used to that. His steel hook was always an object of curiosity and wonder, especially in places where many of the locals had never been in a wheeled vehicle or had seen a TV. To them, a steel hand was indeed most wonderful and strange.

Rossen spoke to Roberto for a minute or two in his best Spanish, then nodded at Tommy.

"Let's go back to the riverbank and see if any word's come down yet."

Heading down the trail, they heard a noise behind them and looked back. They'd picked up two rear guardsmen. Roberto, and Negron, the man with the AK, were following after them. Tommy nodded to no one in particular. It was a good sign.

The sun was like hammers hitting them when they left the sheltering cover of the trees. In just twenty minutes the temperature had climbed as many degrees. The skies were cloudless, clear. On the sandy strip of beach, heat waves rose one after the other to shimmer and dance. Chuck came out of the shade of the black plastic tarp.

"I see you've picked up some company." He greeted Roberto and Negron, then spat out at Tommy and Rossen, "I don't want you to get these guys into any shit, hear me? They're good men and deserve better than you two death merchants have to offer."

Tommy shook his head in resignation. "Chuck, don't you ever change? Is your entire life built around bitching?"

Chuck halted, pursed his lips, nodded his head up and down, his Adam's apple keeping time with the movement. "You know, by God, it *is*. Until the earth is rid of things like you, I guess I'll just have to keep on bitching. Now, would you like a beer?"

Rossen was glad that was over. Tommy was right. Chuck never changed. Ever since they first met in 'Nam he'd been the same. One thing though: You didn't let his outrage-at-violence routine fool you. He was still Special Forces qualified, and besides being a medic was also a light weapons expert and demo man. He wore both the Combat Infantryman's badge and the Combat Medic's and had earned both of them. He was equally proficient with whichever talent was required. Basically, he was a good son of a bitch to have on your side.

"You did say beer, didn't you?"

Chuck pointed back to the hut. "Yeah, I got a couple of Bavarias I had cooling in the river. By

cooling, I mean their temperature is all the way down
to body normal. So let's drink them before they heat
up.''

Chuck opened the bottles. Tommy found a seat on
a pile of small white cargo chutes and settled back to
wait out whatever was going to happen. Chuck and
Rossen walked across the strip to the riverbank. On
the Costa Rican side he could see cleared land with
some brahmalike cattle grazing.

Rossen sat down on a tree stump that had washed
up on the sand.

"Wonder when we're going to hear something?"

Chuck pointed upriver. "There's a regional HQ up
there about two clicks. One of their pongas came by
while you were at the campsites. They said there's a
hell of a fight going on inside. Until that's over, I
wouldn't expect you to know much. Can you tell me
what you're up here for?"

Rossen took a pull of tepid beer, washing it around
his gums. "Yeah, it's no secret. Me and Tomanaga
are going to hold some shooting classes, that's all.
Nothing fancy or spooky about it. Just an easy couple
of weeks training, a paycheck, and back out. That's
it.''

Chuck grunted and squatted on his haunches, Asian
fashion.

"Don't be too sure about that. I've been here
awhile, and they don't bring gringos in to just teach
shooting. If that was all they wanted, they could find
some from South or Central America to do the job.
The only gringos up here besides me are the two
chopper mechanics staying on the Costa Rica side at
Don Felipe's finca. Specialists, that's the only kind
of gringo they'll hire, and we both know what your

specialty is, don't we?'' Chuck had said the last without any rancor. It was just a statement of fact and Rossen took it that way.

The rest of Chuck's statement bothered him. He didn't like games where he didn't know the rules, much less who the players were. Chuck, despite his sometimes frantic approach toward life, was no fool. He saw things and he knew how to analyze them. As soon as he'd see Juliano or Topo, he'd find out just what was coming down. He'd been hired on as a teacher, not as a shooter.

His speculations were broken by the thin whine of an aircraft engine. He started up, getting ready to jack a round in the chamber of his AK. Chuck squinted his eyes and looked to the south.

''Put it down; that's one of ours coming in from Costa Rica. It's the Maule.''

Around the supply hut men began to move, quickly gathering bundles and getting them ready for the aircraft. Cans of gasoline were filled from drums and brought out with hand pumps and funnels, ready to refuel the aircraft.

It came in from the west, following the river course. As it neared, he could see it was painted red and white, not very military colors, but ones less likely to attract attention when flying over neutral countries.

The pilot made an easy landing, throttling back as soon as the wheels touched down, then made a half turn and taxied over to the supply area.

Chuck and Rossen crossed the strip as the pilot and copilot got out, both wearing American-style flight suits.

''Hola, gringo, que tal?''

Rossen responded with: "Hola yourself, Juliano. What's going on?"

"Just a quick turnaround, then we head inside. They need ammo and food pretty bad."

Rossen handed Juliano what was left of his beer. Closing his eyes, the Contra drained the beer in one swallow.

Chuck moved between them. "What about casualties?"

Juliano removed his wraparound sunglasses and wiped them on the sleeve of his flight suit.

"We've got some, Papa Gringo. This afternoon, when we come back from this run, I'm going to go up and try to get into the mountains and bring some out just before dark."

Rossen had to bite his tongue to keep from asking Juliano if he wanted Tommy and him to go along. That wasn't what they had come for.

The plane was fueled and loaded with the bundles wrapped up in the small white drop chutes. Juliano climbed back into the cockpit, made a thumbs-up sign, nodded at his copilot, and started the engine, immediately taxiing to the west, taking off on the same approach he'd made on his landing to take advantage of the breeze coming in from the Atlantic. They'd need all the lift they could get. The plane was badly overloaded and the temperature made the air thin.

Juliano reached the end of the strip, locked his brakes, and revved up the motor to near the red line, then cut loose. The small plane seemed to take a long time getting up to speed, and Rossen caught himself holding his breath, mentally trying to push the overloaded craft into the air. Tommy watched him and knew what he was feeling, even if Rossen didn't know how to verbalize it: He was feeling a sense of guilt for not going with them, a feeling of being left out of something, and he didn't understand it.

Juliano aimed the plane at a small mound of grass. Tommy thought for a second that Juliano was going to have to cut the motor and try again, but the pilot gunned the motor, straining to get enough revs to push the plane up through the thin hot sky. Then it caught and was up and climbing slowly to the starboard until it gained enough altitude. Juliano wagged the wings in salute, then pointed the nose north.

DeCarlo came to stand beside Rossen. "I know. It's always harder to wait and not know what's going on."

It was back to sitting and waiting, or trying to catch a few winks in what shade could be found. Roberto and Negron stayed nearby. Rossen had the feeling they had just been adopted.

Sitting close to Jesús, resting his back against a stack of ammo boxes with American markings, Rossen heard a distant drone. Jesus checked his watch. "It's the day's other commercial flight to San José," he said, and closed his eyes. Rossen kept his open. It was too hot to sleep, and he wasn't tired.

The drone of the aircraft overhead grew stronger, then it became a little thinner. He wondered how Juliano was faring. Then something brought him straight up; he could register just what it was: The droning had changed, it was a sharper tone than before, and stronger. Moving out from the shade of the hut, he looked up. The sharp drone had changed to a nearly high-pitched whine.

Then he saw it coming out of the sun. "Oh, shit!

Tommy, get off your ass and move, we're going to be hit!''

At the same time he heard the cry of *"Avión!"* coming from around the strip. The plane had been spotted by the other Contras and they were scattering. It seemed like a good idea. Grabbing their weapons, Rossen and Tommy headed for cover on the high ground directly behind the supply huts. Looking back, Rossen saw Roberto and Negron jump into a firing pit by the side of the landing strip, their weapons pointed to the sky. Stumbling through the high grass, he passed a shelter and nearly stumbled over an open box. The pitch of the attacking plane was piercing, and he heard the *whoosh* sound of rockets being fired. Rossen hit the deck, covering his head with his arms, and waited. It wasn't long in coming. A bracket of rockets went down each side of the strip. None hit the supply huts.

Rossen wondered what the pilot was thinking. There wasn't any way really to damage a gravel strip with rockets. Whining, red-hot pieces of shrapnel went overhead, cutting through tree branches. Then came machine-gun fire: The plane was strafing! He heard one short scream and saw Chuck dart from cover off to the side of the runway, where he'd carried the little girl. Rossen knew he was going for whoever had been hit.

The pilot cut back on his throttle and the engine sound changed, became deeper, throatier. He was turning to the starboard to make another pass. Standing up, Rossen saw Chuck on the other side of the strip, a Contra on his shoulders, trying to carry him back across the open ground to cover. If the Sandinista pilot made his turn fast enough, Chuck would be caught in the open.

He looked down at the open box by his feet. It had an RPD Russian light machine-gun and a couple of drums of ammo. Grabbing it, he headed back down the strip, Tommy on his tail. As he ran, he fitted a belt in the gun and chambered the first round. Rossen hit the east end of the strip as the plane was making its approach. The pilot had throttled back and began to fire its machine-guns. Working his tail back and forth, the rounds began to close on Chuck. Tommy didn't have to be told what to do. He grabbed the bipod on the light machine-gun and held it above his head, becoming a living gun platform for Rossen. The American's mind took in all the elements like a computer and spat out the desired information: Range, speed, angle of fire, lead time. He squeezed the trigger in ten-round bursts. Every sixth round was a tracer, and using the streak of fire, he walked the bullets to the nose of the attacking plane and held the gun on it as the pilot tried to strafe.

In the cockpit the pilot jerked back in his seat. His windshield shattered as the first bullets hit. Instinctively, he jerked the controls left and banked away off target. More rounds stitched the side of his plane. He didn't like that at all.

Rossen continued to fire. Roberto and Negron were giving them what little help they could, emptying magazines from their weapons as fast as they could fire. Rossen saw Roberto standing up with his M-14, coolly facing the 02, and laying fire on it. Negron was out of the pit in the kneeling position, aiming at the sky. Neither seemed to have any fear of the 02's machine-gun fire hitting them. He could see where a rocket had struck within three feet of the firing pit. Good men!

Chuck made it with his wounded to where he placed the little girl. Rossen turned to face the banking aircraft, his fifty-round belt about gone, when he saw a smoke trail heading for the 02. The plane exploded as the rocket made contact. In an uncontrolled half tailspin, the 02 spun back in, heading down in a wild spiral that looked as if it had been filmed in slow motion. Then it was gone, plunging into the tops of the trees. The explosion that came later rose with gasoline and oil flames over the canopy of the jungle, punctuated by the crackle of exploding machine-gun bullets.

Tommy released his hold on the bipod so Rossen could lower the machine-gun. When he did, he pointed over to where the trail of the RPG-7 rocket had come. Chuck stood there, the empty launcher tube in his hand, swearing. When he'd dropped the wounded Contra, he'd run back to the supply hut and grabbed up an RPG, knowing that it wasn't likely that the 7.62mm rounds in Rossen's light machine-gun could take out the aircraft.

Rossen tossed the pissed-off medic a highball salute, thinking it was not wise to piss off Papa Gringo.

14

Less than an hour later the Maule came back, and Juliano landed and got out, wiping his forehead as he looked around. "I see you've had company."

Jesus told him of the gringos' participation and the end result.

Juliano whistled. That was good, very good. He turned the Maule over to his copilot and told him to take it back across the border, then went over to Rossen and the others. Chuck asked him about the little girl and the wounded man. Juliano looked them over.

"Okay, put them in the plane. The girl will be taken to the Children's Hospital in Costa Rica, and we have a place where the man can get treatment from a surgeon." Chuck picked the girl up, stuffing a piece of paper in her pocket. "If you need anything, you have someone call this number and a big fat gringo man will come to you. He is my friend and will help you. If I can, I will come and see you

131

myself. If I don't make it, it is only because I have much work to do here with the other children. Do you understand?''

She shook her head, trying to fight back tears.

He put her in the seat, secured the belt snugly, and closed the door. Through the Plexiglas, her brown eyes never left his face until the plane taxied away, huge brown eyes that hadn't yet learned to really smile.

Juliano broke up the moment.

"Okay, Papa, you and the others get your gear. We're going downriver a bit, to where the chopper is. I have another run to make. We have some men in bad shape on the mountain. I can make one more run before it gets too dark." To Rossen and Tomanaga he said, "It's best if you come with me, too. If the weather is good, then tomorrow I'll take you in and you can get to work. Also, it will give you a chance to meet our mechanics."

At the riverbank they loaded into a twenty-foot ponga piloted by a black fighter from Bluefields. Skillfully, he swung the nose out in the current, and they headed downstream. It was a short ride. Less than fifteen minutes later they pulled into the bank on the Costa Rican side of the border and clambered up a steep incline where a two-story white clapboard house with a porch stood on the rise overlooking the river. To the left was a corral with half a dozen horses in it, and to the back, behind a couple of strands of barbed wire, they could see a small herd of the big-humped brahmas grazing.

A redheaded man with a fierce mustache and bright eyes greeted them. He looked like a thoroughbred Scot.

Juliano introduced him. "This is Enrique. He works for Don Felipe, whose land this is."

Enrique greeted them in Spanish, hugging Chuck around the shoulders. It was obvious they knew each other well. Enrique did not speak a word of English, but it was true he had the blood of the Scots in him four generations back. It had jumped the line then, cutting out all the Indian and Spanish heritage to leave him as he was, fair-skinned and freckled. He would have been perfectly suited to a set of kilts.

Indicating a hill to the south, Enrique told them the mechanics were up there and Don Felipe would not return till nightfall, or perhaps the next day. He made it clear the newcomers were very welcome, and helped them move their gear inside. Then he excused himself, picking up a chain saw and saying he had work to do in the fields and would return at dark.

Rossen was pleased to see there was a sink with a faucet in a small kitchen. "Hey, Tomanaga, this ain't so bad. We got running water."

Juliano told them to wait there. He would go on to the helicopter and if it was able to fly, he would go into the mountain and should return before nightfall.

"Please be at ease here. These are good friends. If you have any questions, ask Papa; he knows them well. Adios."

Tomanaga looked around. "Well, what now?" Going outside, he saw a couple of lawn chairs and three hammocks stretched out between the posts holding up the porch. "Hey, Chuck, is it okay if I use one of these and get off my feet? I want to enjoy the shade and the breeze."

"Sure, those are company hammocks. Felipe gets a lot of visitors coming and going. You'll like him.

He's a good man. But be careful about Enrique. He is the most energetic son of a bitch I have ever seen. Everything he does is at double time. You know the type—if he asks you if you want a coconut, and you say yes, he'll go out, cut down a tree, and drag it back to you so you can pick out the one you want.''

From behind the hill to the south they heard turbines trying to kick over, then the heavier, throatier hum as it gained rpm's and caught.

Chuck looked that way. A Loach that had seen better days came up over the hill, skimming over the house, heading north across the river.

''Well, there goes Juliano. That is one fine dude. A tough bastard and smart. Rossen, Tomanaga, give these people a chance. I believe in them and I think you will, too. Help them if you can. I don't mean just take their money and do a job. Help them. They need all they can get, desperately. Just give them a chance. . . .''

Chuck's plea was interrupted by a hail.

''Hey there, Papa! Who you got with you? Juliano told us we had company.''

Three men came onto the porch, two gringos and a Latin. The mechanics.

Jerry Sims was sunburned, thin, and had a squint to his eyes that was a heritage from a Cherokee grandmother. A good portion of his head was covered by a full heavy beard and a receding hairline that wouldn't last till he reached forty. Paul Melton, the other gringo, was shorter, more intense-looking, very American, with reddish hair and blue eyes. He had heavy shoulders and strong hands. The last man was introduced by Chuck as Manuel Torres from

Guatemala. He'd been brought in to help the other two with some technical problems on the choppers.

After introductions were finished, Melton settled into one of the lawn chairs and asked, "Anyone want a beer?"

There were no refusals. Sims did the honors, having one time in his many and varied careers been a bartender in Nashville. He announced sardonically, "We got warm Imperial, specialty of the house."

While Sims was gone, Melton said, "One good thing about having an ex-bartender as a partner is they're programmed to get the drinks and empty the ashtrays. Hope he never finds that out."

When the beers were brought out, Sims asked, "What the hell was all that shit going on upriver? Did the periquackos hit the strip again?"

Tomanaga confused, said, "Peri . . . whatos?"

Chuck explained. "Periquackos is what the Contras call the Sandinistas. It's some kind of monkey that's even dumber than most. As for the noise, they hit us again but this time we got us one—the cocksucker went down in flames, as they say. That should slow them up a bit."

Melton had a worried look. "One of these days they're going to cross the river and hit us here. We don't have a damned thing to stop them with. You know, Papa. If they take out these two lousy Loaches we got here, they knock out nearly half of the Contras' resupply capability. I don't like it. We should be farther back inland."

Chuck took a pull of the warm beer, made a face, and replied, "I know it's dangerous for you guys here, but if you were farther inland, as you say, the Costa Ricans would have your asses in a matter of days. Here, if we get word they're coming, we can be across the river in minutes. So that's the way it is.''

Melton reconciled himself, as he did at least twice a day, to the realities of the job.

"Well, if you guys will excuse me, I'm going down to the river and take a bath. I want to wash some of this jet fuel off before it eats my skin away. Anyone else want to go? The water's fine.''

The rest of the afternoon was spent with Rossen and Tomanaga trying to give the others an update on what was happening in the outside world. Torres had gone down to the river with Melton but had taken the ponga to the other side. There was a small Contra camp there, and the kids kept Don Felipe and his household supplied with fish and the monstrous foot-long crawdads that bred in the river.

Torres got back when the shadows were beginning to grow longer. Looking to the north, he said, "Juliano should be back soon. But I worry; you don't know what it's like in there. He has to fly by terrain features, and if the rains set in, then he has to put down. Also, there are the periquacko fighter planes. If they are fighting over the mountain, then it is very tricky. Damn those old machines. They are over-worked, overloaded, and all of them have problems with contaminated fuel.''

While Torres was gone, Sims had filled them in on his background. Manuel Torres had been in Vietnam with the US army as a chopper mechanic, but kept his Guatemalan citizenship. He was the best.

Now Rossen asked Torres if he knew Freddie. He didn't, but he promised to look him up when he got back to Guatemala City the next week. He was going o be here just until the major problems were solved, then Sims and Melton could take over and handle the regular maintenance.

The sun had begun to set, the river turning into a flow of melted gold, when they heard the throb of the Loach's turbine. They all looked to the north except for Chuck, who went inside the kitchen, where he had his medic kit spread out on the table. Lighting a kerosene lamp, he gave the supplies a last look. Satisfied that he had everything he needed—or at least everything available—and at the ready, he went back outside.

Skimming over the treetops from the Nicaraguan side, Juliano brought the Loach in to land forty feet away from the house. One man in uniform got out and began to help three men in the back section. All were wounded. Everyone went to give them a hand. Only one needed to be carried. The other two had shrapnel wounds in their arms and legs, but nothing they were going to die from immediately.

Chuck took over, telling the two walking wounded to find a place and sit down—he'd get to them in a minute.

The stretcher case was another story. He had him taken inside to the kitchen and put gently on the table. Taking the lantern, the medic examined him: There were no visible wounds; the man's skin was dry. Flecks of dried blood spotted his lips, and he was in great pain. As soon as he put his stethoscope to the wounded man's abdomen, Chuck knew what he was facing. Silent stomach and pain on touch: Concussion! The man'd had something burst inside of him, and he had peritonitis.

Tomanaga asked if they could do anything and was

told to get out of the light. Chuck set up an IV from his small stock and began loading the man up with penicillin and streptomycin, making notes of the medication on a tag that he would send along so the doctors at the next stop would know what medication had been given and how much.

He checked the other men. They were in good shape; the medics on the mountain had done a fine job and they weren't in much pain, or at least the pain wasn't anything they couldn't handle by themselves. Good! He needed to save all of his painkillers and anesthetics for the bad cases. It was from them that they found out the man on the table had been hit by a mortar round three days ago, and had gone without any medication until just before Juliano came in to get them. The supplies Juliano had dropped earlier in the day were the first medicines they'd seen in two weeks.

Enrique came back, setting a chain saw down on the porch. He didn't seem surprised by the new arrivals. Pointing up the stairs, he told Chuck to take the walking wounded up, where there were two beds they could have; he would take one of the hammocks outside. The other man would stay on the kitchen table. Chuck didn't want him moved any more than necessary.

With the wounded settled, the rest of them could indulge in the supper Enrique had prepared. Black beans and rice. The half-dozen fish Torres had brought back with him were a welcome addition. Chow done, they found the night full on them. They sat or lay in hammocks on the porch, taking advantage of the night breeze off the river, and talked of the things all men do. Sports and women, booze and women, other jobs and wars, and, of course, women—of which there was a shortage in the zone.

One by one, conversations ended as they fell asleep. Chuck spread a mosquito net over himself and warned the others to do the same.

"Malaria is supposed to be a thing of the past, but don't you believe it." They followed his example; where things like that were concerned, Papa Gringo was usually right.

Before going in to sleep on Don Felipe's bed, Juliano said, "We'll go over in the morning after getting the wounded moved. Sleep well."

Sleeping well didn't seem to be the easiest suggestion to follow.

Rossen didn't like the idea that there were no sentries posted around the farmhouse. It didn't seem right, but so far the Sandinistas had stayed on their side of the river and this section, for a distance of twenty miles in either direction, was under the control of the ARDE Contras.

15

Rossen *didn't* sleep well that night. He was still not used to spending so much time in a hammock, monkeys raising hell in the treetops, bats flying around slaughtering God knows what kind of bugs, and then there was the snoring. Chuck had gone into a spell of nasal symphonies that led Rossen at one time to giving serious consideration to stuffing his hammock up the man's sinus cavities.

Several times he'd gotten up, walked around, listened for a time, then lay back in the hammock to sleep a few more minutes before some new sound jerked at his gritty eyes, his hand reaching for his AK-47. It was going to take a while before all the noises sorted themselves out and he could let his subconscious determine which were natural and for which he should awaken.

Dawn did come at last, and Rossen could give up thinking about sleep.

Chuck took the wounded in the ponga to the landing strip to wait for the next plane to come in and take them out. His parting words to them had been: "You guys are going in with Juliano today, so I'm going to say adios and get on about my business. Once I get these guys taken care of, I've got a small camp upriver, where most of the refugee kids that need help come. I've been gone too long. So, remember what I said yesterday."

They promised to stop in if they had a chance and walked to the bank to wave good-bye. He was a good man, even if he did still suffer from having ideals. One day they'd get him killed.

Watching a low bank of clouds coming inland in waves from the Atlantic side, Juliano said, "It should clear up in a few minutes. You wait here and I'll take the Loach back over the hill and get her fueled up. I would have done it last night, but I don't like flying that thing at night; it has problems even for a short distance."

Sims and Melton went with him, and Torres stayed behind with Rossen and Tomanaga.

Airborne, Juliano used the radio on the Loach to contact Topo.

"All right, I'll take them to the training camp right now and tell them they will have to wait to meet the *comandante*. . . . Yes, I think you are right, we should save him till he is needed. Very good. I will check in later."

Walking back over the hill, Juliano told the two to get their things and follow him back to where the Loach was being serviced.

"I am to take you on to the training camp and let you get settled in. Right now the weather is bad inside, so you will have to wait a bit to meet our leader. Is that all right with you?''

Neither Rossen nor Tomanaga had any problems with it. They didn't see any real need to meet the *comandante* anyway. They'd made their deal and would live up to it. But it did seem that things went rapidly from one direction to another around here.

''No, there's no problem, and we'd just as soon get to work.''

Juliano pointed at the Loach. ''Get in and we'll move out.''

Sims and Melton moved away from the chopper blades, telling Juliano, ''Keep an eye on the temperature, and for Christ sake remember—it's a helicopter, not a dive bomber; it can't take the strain.''

Juliano gave them a thumbs-up, put on his helmet, and hit the starter.

Once in the air, Rossen had his first good look at the country. It was beautiful. Primal rain forest, much of it what they called triple-canopy. Flocks of birds broke cover constantly: herons, cranes, parrots, and macaws. Several times they passed over trees that were the homes of tribes of monkeys. When the helicopter passed, they swarmed out on the branches, leaping and jumping in panic at the flight of the monstrous bird flapping overhead. From one tree to another they fled, seeking security from the unknown.

The river was their guide for about forty miles. They followed it downstream, then turned to the north to fly low over forests and swamps. This was flatter land than where they had been. Mangrove swamps and marshes ran for hundreds of miles, and on the maps and charts of the world much of it was marked ''unexplored.''

They had no idea where they were when Juliano sighted on some unknown landmarks and made a bank to the left, heading west for a short time, then once more to the north, and began to bring the Loach down.

The training camp in no way resembled a vacation resort. It was basic. Thatched huts set under the cover of the trees, a few cleared patches of land for a rifle range, and the jungle itself for field training.

A small crowd of Contras gathered around the Loach as it set down, eager hands reaching up to help with any gear or supplies to be taken off. Rossen handed down his pack and was surprised to see himself looking into the dark, squinting eyes of Roberto, with Negron standing right behind him.

Rossen looked at Juliano, who just shrugged his shoulders. "They must have come down after you left the airstrip yesterday, then marched all night through the jungle. I guess they want you to teach them."

Tomanaga grinned. He liked the idea and he liked the two Indians. "Good enough, they're our first pupils."

Juliano introduced them to the camp commander, Antonio Montenegro, a swarthy mulatto with a huge oily black beard that hung in waves to his chest. He was an impressive and robust man, who carried an Israeli Uzi in a shoulder holster and an AK with a folding stock in his hand. Both looked like toys on him.

They were greeted profusely. Roberto and Negron had already told the camp of their coming and of the attack at the airstrip. They were welcomed as compadres: friends and comrades.

Juliano never got out of the Loach. "This is as far as I go. Antonio will take care of you. He has orders to give you all that you need or at least all that we have. Do as you wish. I will see you again. Until then, train us some good shooters, we need them. There is much dying to be done, and we prefer it to be the periquackos and not us. Good-bye and *buena suerte*, amigos."

He took off, leaving them standing in the jungle surrounded by curious brown and black faces.

Tomanaga put his pack on his shoulder, ignoring the looks at his claw. "Well, let's get to it."

And they did. They had good assistants in Negron and Roberto, as well as several others who had been with the Sandinistas until they'd defected.

For the next four weeks they ran constant training cycles in basic marksmanship and quick-kill techniques of fire. From the classes they picked the best to be trained as instructors, and later as snipers. Life was spartan but good. Both men liked being back in the field, and they liked the people they worked with. As Chuck had said, "Give them a chance."

They heard little from anyone during those four weeks. An occasional greeting by radio from Juliano, or Chuck, who was working with his kids and happier than a dead hog in the sunshine, or from Topo, who filled a few requests they made for some custom loads for the rifles. When they wanted some Sionic sound suppressors as well as night-sight devices, they were provided.

At the end of the fifth week they had a visitor. The *comandante*, Eden Pastora, came to see them.

He was on the short side, but impressive. Like Montenegro, he sprouted a lush black beard. Once he et foot on the ground, Rossen and Tomanaga knew he was the man Chuck had said he was. His troops warmed about him. He was the father image. He touched one's arm here, gave an embrace to another one there, knowing everyone's name. He was immaculate. His camouflage uniform and weapons were spotless. That was hard to find; someone who could stay clean in a jungle war was a hell of a dude.

When Montenegro brought Rossen and Tommy to him, he was gracious, distant, and polite. He'd had a request from Topo and was to put it to the gringos. He liked the idea, mainly because Topo was a sly and devious devil. His idea was sound, and as the Americans would say, it was also cost-effective.

He invited Rossen to eat with him that evening, just the two of them. A good dinner in honor of his coming; several of the camp chickens and a pig would be sacrificed to do the occasion justice.

Showing up at the hut the *comandante* had taken for the evening, Rossen set his rifle by the door under the watchful eyes of the *comandante*'s bodyguards. Entering, he was invited to sit. Scotch was brought out. Rossen took a glass; Pastora had mango juice. He didn't drink alcohol very often.

Rossen knew when he was in the presence of a natural leader. He was drawn to the man. And he believed what he was told that night of the struggle and how Pastora saw the future of his country and the importance of Central America to the rest of the world, especially to the United States. Without taking another drink, Rossen knew that he'd been had when he left the *comandante*'s hut and returned to his own. He'd been had, but he didn't mind it.

He found Tomanaga leaning back against a banana palm.

"You know, Tommy, that is a hell of a man in there. I don't know how, but I think I just got us into something else. I knew I should have let you go in."

Tomanaga just grinned. "He didn't want me; he wanted you. Maybe he knew that being Japanese, I have a more practical and intelligent approach toward life. But if you make a deal, then we'll do it. Does it really make any difference?"

Rossen sat beside him and slapped him hard on the shoulder. "No, I don't guess it does. But I'm not sure you're going to like this."

16

What the fuck am I doing here? Lowering the rifle from his shoulder, Rossen wiped his eyes with the back of his hand. *I'm getting too old for this shit. So why? This was supposed to be just a training job. I know Pastora conned me into this, but I'll bet that it was Topo who put him up to it.*

He nudged Tommy to take over the watch, handing him the M-14 with the Starlight. There was no need for words; they had worked together too long for that. Tomanaga adjusted his position, getting as comfortable as possible, letting the tree log in front of him bear the weight of the rifle as he centered on the road.

Rossen rolled over to his back, closing his eyes and wanting a smoke. That was another thing. He smoked too much now. Before, it had never bothered him to go without one. Clenching his eyes tightly, he rubbed a sore spot behind his shoulder blade. Cock-

ing an ear, he listened. It was fairly quiet. Maybe the
animals knew they were there. No! That's not it. In
the past, when people were around, the damned howler
monkeys would go crazy with their *whump whump*
all night long. You could hear one of them for miles,
but when they got together in packs, it could make
you crazy.

His stomach gave a tentative gurgle. Too many
days of nothing but black beans and rice or, if you
wanted a change, you got rice and black beans. At
least they didn't give you gas the way navy or pinto
beans did. Small consolation. . . .

It would be light soon and they'd switch over to
the ART, the adjustable ranging telescope. From his
left he heard a soft snore stop suddenly as Negron cut
off Roberto's breath with his hand. *Good man.
That's the way. Keep it quiet.*

Not much in the way of a formally trained backup
team, but they were steady, good men. Both of them
Miskito Indians with just a touch of Spanish blood,
for whom this was not a war of political philoso-
phies, but one of religion.

The Sandinistas had started fucking around with
Mother Church, and for men like these, that was too
much. Rossen didn't care why they were fighting
the Sandinistas; he was just glad they were, at least
for the time being, on his side. They were tough men
in their late forties. Fighters. Soldiers.

There was a slight chill, more from dampness than
from the lowering temperature. A shiver ran up
Rossen's spine and down his shoulders once, twice,
then no more.

He wished he hadn't told Juliano about the way the
Viet sniper had tied up entire convoys for days. Then

the bastard wanted a practical demonstration. Rossen had protested, but Juliano had upped the ante considerably for the demonstration. Money! But he knew that wasn't all of it. He still needed this and didn't know why. Maybe if he'd had more time with the shrink in 'Nam, he could have found out, but would finding out make any difference? Maybe Tommy had it right. He'd said they were dinosaurs looking for their tar pit. An animal trying to become extinct, not really wanting to continue, but not having the balls to kill themselves. So they would keep going till someone else did it for them. Who knows? He was still here, and if it wasn't here, it would have been somewhere else. He peered over at Tommy and grinned in the darkness. Tommy's left hand was covered in a homemade camouflage glove to conceal the shine of his stainless steel claw. Good man. Makes it a bit easier having him around. It never used to, but it does now.

He pulled back the flap on his watch. 0447. The Sandinistas or Cuban chopper pilots would be heading out to the flight line about now to begin their regular morning patrol along the edge of the jungle and to give cover to the outgoing convoy. There was a rise on the road about a click and a half away; if he were on it, he would have been able to see the lights of Rama in the distance. If the periquackos kept to their schedule, they'd pull out at about 0600 and reach his position at approximately 0715. A short time, but a long wait. His palms began to sweat.

This was the last one. He'd hit two convoys in succession, killing the lead drivers, then bugging out. The first one didn't bother the Sandinistas very much; they just figured it was an isolated attack of no importance. Snuffing the lead driver on the next convoy the following day probably started making them a bit edgy, and this third one would definitely get their shit in an uproar. It should be getting tough to find volunteer drivers about now. When he pulled out, he'd leave his two back-up men as the shooters. They were the best of the lot. Good, solid, patient, and without too much imagination. They would be able to wait the hours and days not moving, not speaking. Always, he emphasized that all they needed to do was to kill the lead driver any way they could and that it wasn't always by shooting: a mine in the road, blow a bridge when it was being crossed. A grenade tossed in the window when the truck had to slow up around a curve. Any way! But always kill the lead driver. Three or four more and they'd have to force men into the lead seat at gunpoint, which naturally had a less than uplifting effect upon the morale of the men involved and would rapidly decrease the popularity of the officers who gave the orders.

The mist was rising now from the jungle floor, floating softly up as the earth began to warm with the approach of dawn. Right now it rested gently, barely moving. A thick blanket that would thin and rise up into the leaves and branches of the jungle when the sun was properly up.

Snapping his fingers, he motioned for the Miskitos to get in position. Tommy adjusted his body and the log serving as a rest for his weapon. The Starlights were exchanged for the ART. To their rear was the river, to the east the new road to Bluefields, where the airstrip was being lengthened to take fighters.

Rama, once a typical sleepy village, was being expanded as a supply center and support base for operations from the Atlantic side. From the depots there, material was trucked over land to Bluefields or put on flat-bottomed barges to float down the river if the waters weren't too rough or swollen by the monsoon rains, as they were now.

A fluttering at the back of his mind brought his eyes up. The day was light enough to see for about two hundred meters without any aids. The mist had risen above the trees to about three hundred feet. The fluttering increased in intensity. The others heard and were still.

Then it came into sight. An olive-drab Hind-A assault chopper. He knew it was loaded for bear and maybe a bear was piloting the thing, a Russian or Cuban bear. The Hind came over just under the rising mist. Eyes on board would be searching the wall of the jungle lining the road. The thickest growth had been cut back about fifty meters on both sides to give those on the convoys a bit more protection from ambush . . . and time to tell from where hostile fire was coming.

The chopper passed on, heading to the east. Rossen checked his weapon one more time, wiped the lens of the scope to clear it of any condensation, and adjusted the focus. A round was already in the chamber, as it had been all night, but now the safety was taken off. The small hairs at the back of his neck and on his forearms rose in anticipation. They were coming. . . .

The lead vehicle snuck its nose over the rise and headed for them. A Russian UAZ-66, a jeeplike vehicle but a bit bigger than the American counterpart. Its windshield was down and an LMG mounted where the passenger-gunner had a clear field of fire.

In the back were two other passengers, who eyed the ominous dark of the jungle. They didn't like being the point men. They were basically city boys from Managua; the jungle meant nothing good for them.

Negron and Roberto adjusted their position so as to be able to keep an eye on the road. If after the gringo killed the lead driver those in the little Russian car were stupid enough to come back and offer assistance . . . They hoped they were . . . it was not fair for the gringo to have all the fun.

The jeep passed them. Through his scope Rossen could see the worry and concentration lines on the driver's face. The last two killings hadn't been enough to stop the convoys or modify their movements, but it was enough to start the edge of fear working on those who had to drive the narrow road.

The grinding sound of the truck's shifting gears made him swing his scope around. The jeep passed out of sight three hundred meters in front of the lead truck. Tommy had not moved his scope; he was waiting expressionless, showing no sign of tension. He had detached his mind from everything but the road and the targets that were approaching. It was his way: If he ever started thinking, he wasn't sure what would happen.

The lead truck came on, painted in the Soviet version of olive drab. Inside the cab the driver cursed the truck—the transmission had been giving him problems. He geared down, picked up a little speed, then shifted into a higher range. Fingering the trigger guard of his AKA, his shotgun rider kept his eyes on his side of the road, glaring at the wall of greenery as though it were a personal enemy out to do him harm.

Behind the lead truck came two more, then another

UAZ with the convoy commander, Captain Morales, in the passenger seat, holding the hand phone to his radio. So far so good: Neither the MI-8 or point vehicle had anything to report. Their patrols, which swept the area early this morning, had likewise reported nothing. The area was clear. The last two attacks had been nothing more than a futile attempt to harass them. The Contras were not strong enough, or stupid enough, to stay in the area for this long. They would be long gone by now. Back to their safe camps across the Rio San Juan, where they could plot and talk and do very little else.

Rossen focused on the face of the driver, then dropped to the junction of the throat—that small hollow where doctors insert breathing tubes. The windshield shouldn't make too much difference. He'd fire two rapid shots, letting the natural rise of the second place his shot in the face of the driver. The pleasant, slightly sweet smell of thin gun oil tickled the hairs in his nostrils; it reminded him of some kind of candy he'd eaten long ago as a child. Not aware of exactly when it was taking place, his finger began taking up the trigger slack. It knew within a thousandth of a pound exactly how much pressure to apply. The weapon was ready, the shooter was relaxed, and his breathing had become easy, stopping the beginning of a nervous tremor in his legs. Concentrate, always concentrate. The driver's face loomed larger. Now he was at three hundred meters. An easy shot, but he waited until the truck made a light curve that brought it face on to him. Then he let instinct take over, releasing conscious thought to it. Reflexes developed by years and thousands of hours took over. He didn't select the time to fire; his entire body did.

Acting of its own accord, it knew when it was right and he had learned long ago to listen to it.

Morales stood up in the seat of his jeep as it crested the rise in order to get a better look at the road in front of him. His three leading trucks were well spaced out, not bunched together. In the back of each were armed men ready to respond to any ambush. Behind him came a gift from their brothers in socialism, a tracked BMD Light Armored fighting vehicle mounting a 30mm cannon and carrying six heavily armed soldiers in the rear, and behind it the remaining six vehicles of the transport column, one filled with soldiers protected by sheets of boiler plate and sandbags on the truckbed in case of mines.

The windshield exploded: Through the scope Rossen saw the glass disintegrate; the second round was off before the face of the driver had time to register the first bullet hitting him on the Adam's apple. The second round took him in the face just to the right of his nose.

Tommy took out the shotgun rider with two shots through the side of the door. The truck careened off the side of the road, settling in a ditch. Behind it, the others came to screeching stops as brakes were locked, and drivers wondered what they should do. There was no way to reverse without running into one of their own trucks.

Rossen didn't wait to see what they would do. Now came the part he hated: the running. The chopper would not be reluctant to pursue them over the jungle, this neck of the woods was still in their hands. He slid out of his cover and led the way, followed by Tommy. Roberto and Negron had another job to do. They were to draw the enemy off, then follow. It made sense: Try as they might, he and Tommy couldn't match the Indians in speed or silence traveling through the jungle. Now they had to run and evade the enemy until morning; then, if the weather permitted, Juliano and his old Loach would be in to get them out. From all around them came sounds of confusion and panic. The birds had been stirred up and were squawking and screeching their protests. Random rifle fire from the troops in the rear of the trailing trucks sprayed the tree line. He thought he heard a familiar grinding sound, but he wasn't sure; tanks weren't much used around here. Then came a muted thump. A 30mm round landed somewhere to his right.

17

"Let's get the hell out of here!"

Tommy needed no further encouragement. He was hot on Rossen's ass. It was simple. Just run as fast as you could and try not to get your feet tangled in the undergrowth. They had a two-hundred-yard sprint through the trees and brush before they hit the animal trail that led to the south. In this kind of terrain the enemy would be lucky if they could find the trail in an hour, if they found it at all; by that time they should be able to break contact.

Morales screamed for his men to counterattack. They moved smartly, leaving the trucks and heading straight into the jungle, firing as they went. They didn't hit much, but it sounded good. Negron and Roberto stayed where they were, letting the periquackos move past them.

Morales stayed on the road, yelling into his radio

for the Hind and for the front scout car to return and give them assistance. To the Hind he radioed the direction from which the shots had come and which way he thought the snipers were heading. Morales wanted the ambushers.

Chests heaving, Rossen and Tommy hit the animal trail and followed the narrow path, twisting and dodging. Overhead the trees formed a canopy of deep shimmering green. As long as they stayed under them, there was little chance the crew of the Hind helicopter would spot them. The only problem was that the trail ended a half mile south, and then they had a field to cross that was nearly a half mile wide. The only "cover" there was the waist-high grass. If the Sandinistas were able to locate them in it, and the chopper pilot knew what he was doing, they could be in deep shit.

Behind them they heard gunfire popping like firecrackers in the distance. Negron and Roberto were doing their best to draw off the pursuers. Rossen wished them luck in their efforts, but a rattle of automatic fire through the tree branches over his head, followed by a rain of splinters and leaves, said that there wasn't much likelihood they would be successful. Morales had had a bit of blind luck. Two of his men had worked in this area and knew it quite well, including where the animal trails were and how far it was to the open field to the south.

Rossen bent over and pushed forward faster, Tommy hot on his tail. The brush was so thick that it wasn't a good spot to set up and get off a few shots to slow the Sandinistas down. If they were able to get across the field, he would be able to try something, but not now . . . it was too close.

Ahead the trail lightened. They were near the field. If there'd been any other tactic, they wouldn't have done it this way, but they had no choice. Their options were even worse to either flank, where they'd end up in swamps. This was the only way out. Gulping down lungfuls of air, they halted for a second to look and listen behind them and to the front. From the rear, the crashing of branches, curses, and warnings in Spanish decided matters for them once and for all. They hit the clearing as fast as they could, weaving through the high grass, trying to get as much lead on their enemy as possible. Near the center of the clearing was a small grove of trees. It was time to play leapfrog.

"Tommy, you get on across and set up and I'll give them some shit from here. Then you cover me when I break for it."

Tommy nodded, saving his wind for the distance still ahead of him. It would take him at least four minutes to cover the remaining ground. Four lousy minutes. Time was never fair. Rossen shinnied up in the branches of one of the trees set back a bit from the front. The branches were thick enough to give his camouflage some effect and break up his body outline but still thin enough for him to be able to pick targets. On a branch the size of his thigh about twenty feet off the deck, he settled into a semblance of the squatting position. Resting his elbows on his knees, he adjusted his scope. He knew the distance to the tree line from which the Sandinistas would have to break. They were channeled by the same terrain features he and Tommy were.

*   *   *

Morales was coming up behind his lead elements, whipping them on and trying to keep a running dialogue going with the Hind as he did. The Hind would be on site in less than a minute. Once that happened, Morales would have the snipers pinned down from the ground and air. He knew the Hind had sensing devices that could aid in locating the fleeing killers.

Rossen was as ready as he was going to be, and the name of the game was to buy time. At the edge of the clearing the first of the Sandinistas halted and crouched, looking in all directions. The distance was about four hundred meters, and Rossen had him dead center in the ART. No way to miss. But he waited. He wanted to lay it on. Let some more move out into the open.

Four more joined the first one. They stood making signs, arguing about who was going to enter the clearing first. Rossen thought he made out, by the hand motions in the shadows of the trees, a figure giving orders but couldn't be sure. He wished that whoever it was giving orders would come out to where he could get a shot at him; that would be the best thing he could hope for right now. He waited but the man didn't break cover and then the Sandinistas were starting to move across the field and Rossen had to do the job before they got spread out.

Rapidly, he came on to his first target, the sequence already picked out. Letting his mind go off somewhere into the distance, he gave his body over to pure reflex. The rifle bucked against his shoulder.

He didn't wait to see if he'd made a hit; he knew he had. The rifle was already on the next target before the first man went down, his back torn open at the spine. The second round was off. Rossen knew this was a hit in the belly. That was good. Screaming men took some of the courage out of their comrades. Another round—he let this target hold it in the face.

The rest hit the ground, seeking what cover they could find, squirming close to the earth and hoping the high grass would keep the shooter's eyes from *him* and he'd pick another target. Three men killed in as many seconds. Morales took cover behind a tree, staying in the shadows. The rest of his men were catching up to him. Those with him were now something less than eager to venture out into the clearing. Morales was not stupid: He knew where the shots were coming from, but he also knew that the shorter range of his men with the AKAs made it unlikely that they would do much damage. Unless he was willing to accept a great many more casualties, the sniper had the best of it for now.

Looking back over his shoulder, Rossen saw Tommy hunkered over, making for the far tree line. Another minute or two and he'd be there. Just beyond that strip of trees was a creek, another patch of jungle, then another clearing, where they were supposed to be picked up at high noon. That was, of course, providing the Loach could get off the ground and that the weather on the way in wasn't so bad they had to abort the flight. Anyway you looked at it, the shit was getting a bit sticky.

Morales gave the Hind pilot hell, threatening him with a firing squad if he didn't get his aircraft on target immediately.

Rossen took out another one with a leg shot. At this point he would just as soon wound as kill. The more wounded casualties he inflicted, the more necessary to take care of them, and the less to be on his ass.

He had just started to scope out the shadows at the edge of the trees to see if he could get a shot off at whoever was giving the orders, when a noise like that of a whirlwind brought an instant pucker to his asshole. A dark, menacing olive-drab shape filled his scope. The Hind! *Oh! shit, I'm in for it now.* He brought the scope onto the pilot's blurred figure and fired. The round bounced. He had thought it would. There was no way he could take out the Hind with an M-14, and right now he was fresh out of SAMs. The Hind rose higher, taking its time. Rossen knew the pilot was playing with him, letting him sweat. On board the helicopter were heat sensors that probably had him zeroed, and Russian versions of the chain gun ready to turn the entire patch of trees he was nesting in into splinters in less than five seconds. If he hit the deck, it wouldn't be much—if any—better. He heard Tommy firing, trying to draw the armored dragonfly off him. It did no good. He was caught!

The noise of the chopper's blades seemed to be coming in stereo, surrounding him. A roar deafened him. He thought for an instant that he'd been hit. Then the Hind exploded in gouts of flame and smoke, fishtailing into the jungle. A shadow passed over him. One of the Contra Loaches. Rocket pods protruded from the runners like wasps' nests. Another barrage of 2.75s rammed into the Sandinistas at the tree line. He unassed his perch and hit the deck, racing for Tommy. The Loach made two more passes, expending all of its ordnance, and whipped back around, flying close to the earth. It settled between Rossen and Tommy, who wasted no time in running out to meet it. Clambering in, Tommy continued to give off random fire, not expecting to hit anything, but hoping to keep the Sandinistas' heads down until Rossen could get on board.

"Give me a hand and let's get the hell out of here!"

Tommy grabbed Rossen's kit and weapon, then grabbed his friend's arm and hauled him up inside the rear of the Loach, ignoring Rossen's screaming protests. "Not with the claw, stupid. Not with the fuckin' claw!"

Juliano never turned around, he just took the mobile little bird off at treetop level as fast as he could, heading back for the relative safety of the San Juan.

Rossen and Tommy sat on the decking, hearts pounding wildly, trying to catch their breath and let legs and arms stop shaking. That had been much too close. Juliano pointed to the extra headset hanging from the cabin. Putting it on, Rossen began yapping at the Latin pilot.

"Where the hell did you come from?"

Juliano grinned. "We came early. The weather forecast was bad, so we came in and sat down at the LZ. I heard what was happening on the radio. One thing the Cubans have never learned is radio security. They just broadcast in the clear and we get their frequencies nearly as fast as they do. So I just hopped over, and there the thing was. I couldn't miss. I don't think he ever saw me. He was having too much fun playing with you."

"Where did you get the rockets? I didn't know you had any."

"We don't tell you everything, gringo. But these just came in and your gringo mechanics worked all night getting them set up. We didn't even have time to test them and see if they worked right or not. But I guess they're okay."

Rossen agreed with him and relayed to Tommy what had come down. Then, yelling into the mouthpiece, he asked, "How long till we get home?"

"I don't know. The weather is still in front of us. We might have to sit down and wait it out. It might not be a bad idea to do that anyway. By now there should be a flight after us from Bluefields or Managua, and I don't think we'll be so lucky two times in a row."

Beneath them the earth moved rapidly. Juliano was keeping the old bird close to the treetops, where they'd be hard to track on radar. But there was only one direction to go home in, and the Sandinistas knew what it was. Their aircraft were also better equipped for foul weather than the Loach.

"You might be right, Juliano. If the Sandinistas have sent some birds after us, we won't have much time before they're on our ass. Maybe we should look for somewhere to hole up for a while."

Juliano nodded and took the Loach up to three thousand feet. "Start looking, shooter. If you see any place, let me know." He turned off the intercom and went back to where he could monitor the enemy's calls. In less than a minute he reopened the intercom.

"Find a place and find it fast, gringo. Our cousins are on the way and they are pissed."

To the southeast Tommy spotted a hole in the canopy of the jungle and pointed it out to the copilot, who showed it to Juliano, who agreed, and swung the small chopper over, heading straight for it and dropping altitude. At treetop level he went into a hover and slowly, ever so gently, lowered the helicopter into the hole, settling it nearly to the ground, then tilting the nose forward slightly and easing the Loach under a concealing roof of branches and thick fat green leaves. From the air they would be invisible. Rossen and Tommy could only sit and watch the blades of the Loach coming within inches of tree branches. If they'd even touched one . . .

Juliano cut the engines and took off his helmet.

"Okay, smoke 'em if you got 'em. We wait now. If they don't locate us in the next half hour, they won't find us ever. A storm front is moving straight for us. So we just sit tight till it passes.

"By the way, from what we've heard, you are beginning to upset some people in Managua and Cuba. Today's action should really tee them off.

Good work, and Topo sends you his personal thanks and congratulations.''

"I'd rather he'd sent a bottle of scotch," Tomanaga grumbled.

"No sooner said than done.'' From his flight bag, Juliano removed a full, unopened bottle of Johnnie Walker Red. "In a way, it's too bad you got out. If you hadn't, then I was going to drink the whole thing in your memory, and you know how expensive this stuff is.''

Rossen took it from him and cracked the top, taking the first long pull. The smoky burning was good as it seared its way down into the pit of his tight stomach and settled into a comforting glow. Tommy was next. Juliano and his copilot observed the diminishing levels of the bottle with alarm until at last he reached back and took it from the still sucking lips of the steel-clawed Japanese.

"Don't be greedy. I think we deserve at least one taste for our small services.''

There was no way Tommy or Rossen was going to argue with that. Juliano had pulled them out. Right now he could have anything he wanted.

18

"You want us to do *what*?"

Topo ignored the outburst, taking it as an expected part of the gringo nature. "It is very simple, my friends. You have met the *comandante* and know how important he is not only to us, but to the world. There have been too many attempts on his life, and they are all directed by these two men, Guzman and the Russian animal, Rasnovitch. I think it only fair that we strike back. Such an act would surely give them pause to reflect on their actions in the future. You men could be the instrument that brings salvation to this part of the world. Think upon it. Not many men have that chance for greatness."

Rossen growled. "Knock off the soft soap, Topo. That kind of bullshit doesn't play. You're right about one thing though: Pastora is too important to let him get his ass blown up without a fight." He glanced over at Tomanaga for a reaction, and got a nod.

"All right. We'll go for it. Now, what kind of plan did you have in mind?"

"I have, in anticipation of your being agreeable to this matter, already put certain steps into motion. Juliano will brief you. Now"—he rose—"if you will excuse me, I have another appointment and many things to take care of in order to prepare for your departure day after tomorrow."

Topo left the room quickly, before Rossen or Tomanaga could respond. He chuckled as he passed the luscious Rosalia, with her hot fanatic eyes. Maybe he would give her to the gringo shooter when he came back. That would certainly teach him which was the more dangerous kind of encounter.

As to the actual operation, he'd had some other thoughts on the way that it should progress, and the best manner of achieving maximum effectiveness from it. He had come across the account of a German SS colonel, Otto Skorzeny. The Allied command thought the SS man was going to try to assassinate Eisenhower. Topo was using Skorzeny's plan as his blueprint. But he did not want his men killed or captured, which was why he had given Juliano orders to break off the mission if anything at all went wrong. They were to return without delay and make no further attempts on the lives of Guzman or Rasnovitch.

No, they would wait for Rosalia. He still had more work for his foreign guests. Until the last job had been completed, he would have to take very good care of them. Then and only then would he consider releasing them to the attentions of his lovely and ballbusting secretary.

He had to make some calls now, to assure every-

thing would go as planned. Downstairs, he called
Rosalia in. There might be one small service she
could perform.

Juliano uncovered his prize. A mint-condition Russian Gaz jeep. Inside were the uniforms he'd ordered. Taking the uniforms and the bagged Russian
weapons out of the jeep, Rossen and Tommy loaded
their gear into the back of the vehicle, covering it
with a tarp. Their Contra camouflage was quickly
stripped off and replaced with new issue. Rossen felt
odd putting on the uniform of a Russian colonel. He'd
never been an officer, never wanted to be. Tommy
grinned his usual impossible-to-determine-what-it-
means grin and buttoned the conservatively cut tunic
that identified him as a *Dai Uy*, a captain in the
People's Army of Vietnam. Juliano swore beneath
his breath as he put on his uniform; that's what it had
been, his. A major in the Sandinista air force. Getting the belt buckled, he adjusted the pistol holster.

"You know, I still don't like this kind of shit. I'm
not a spook, and this is spook business." Rossen's
voice revealed his barely controlled anger.

Tomanaga jacked a round in the chamber of his
AKM. "You might as well knock off the bitching,
shooter. You know we're going to do it, so let's just
get on with it and get out."

"Okay, Tommy, but this is the last gig you book
me into. I'll find the jobs from now on."

Tomanaga climbed into the back seat of the jeep,
settling his thinning haunches on the hard cushions.
"You dumb long nose, you couldn't find work as a
BB-gun instructor if it wasn't for me."

Juliano cautioned them, "From now on, be care-

ul. Do not speak English where any can hear. If you
do, then we will die. Rossen, if we run into any
inquisitive guards, let me do the talking as much as
possible. If they give me too much trouble, you just
jump in and act mad as hell, lots of arm-waving. Not
very many have had my benefits: an education at
Patrice Lumumba University in Moscow. They're
scared shitless of Russians.

"Tomanaga, you keep your weapon ready to fire.
Now, let's get on with it. There are people waiting
for us."

Getting into the front passenger seat, Rossen undid
the flap on his holster and checked to see how tightly
it held the pistol.

"I still don't like it. There's too many holes in the
plan. What if we get ambushed by our own people on
the way into Managua?"

Juliano started the motor. "I told you. All Contras
have been pulled back from this area. We'll have no
trouble till the first checkpoint. Then there'll be one
or two more after entering the city limits. After that,
who knows?

"You know, Rossen, Tomanaga told me that your
code name in Vietnam was Iceman. Well, act like it.
This is important. Do this right and you'll be out of
the country and on your way to wherever you want to
go in forty-eight hours. If it gets fucked up, we'll
probably be buried in about the same time."

Juliano pulled out onto the dirt track that would
take them to the main highway and Managua. At the
far end of the track, in a clearing barely big enough
for the blades of the Loach to spin, was their only
way out. They'd camouflaged it so it couldn't be
seen from the air, and it was unlikely that anyone

would just stumble onto it. At least that was the hope.

Tomanaga leaned forward toward Juliano. "Don't worry about Rossen. He's just letting off steam. You just get us to where we can set up and leave the rest to us. The job'll get done."

Twisting and weaving, the jeep ground its way out of the jungle accompanied by the cries of protesting birds. They had the windshield up to keep branches and vines hanging over the trail from hitting them in the face, and Rossen kept his eyes peeled for any sign of trouble.

It took more than a half hour before they reached the point where the jungle gave way, and ahead of them, just out of sight, was the highway. Tomanaga jumped out of the jeep and ran forward to where he could get a look both ways. He waited, listened, waited again. Five minutes, ten. Two cars passed heading west. Waving Juliano on, Tommy hopped into the back as the Gaz trundled forward, its wheels slipping on the morning-mist-slick grass and finally gripping the blacktop.

Shifting into a higher gear, Juliano settled back. He hated this nearly as much as his passengers did. He hated the uniform and he hated Russians. In some ways he almost hated Rossen and Tomanaga. That they should have to use foreigners to do their killing for them didn't sit well with him. This was his *war,* not some game for hirelings.

He bit his tongue, knowing he was unfair. It was they who had changed the game plan for Rossen and Tomanaga. They had lived up to their end of the bargain. More than lived up to it. Maybe he felt a bit guilty and was taking it out on them because it was the Contras who had suckered them in and now it was more than likely they would be killed. No, he didn't hate them.

He knew that what they were doing was not all for money. He'd seen them too many times with the men and villagers and, of course, there was always the crazy one, Papa Gringo. They were just men who had lost their reasons for living and looked now, perhaps, for some meaning in death.

Several trucks with Sandinistas in them passed them heading east. They were waved at by the soldiers, who shouted brave slogans. Juliano's face hardened at the sound of them. Rossen just kept looking ahead, his face showing nothing. He was exercising all of his control. This was different. He wanted to be back in the jungle. That he knew and understood. This was a different kind of pressure. The tension was all inside, and you couldn't let any of it out. He looked around over his shoulder. Tomanaga sat as if half asleep. Rossen knew he wasn't by the way his trigger hook was lightly stroking the safety on his AKM.

Rossen ran over the plan in his mind again. It was simple enough on the surface. This Guzman was their first target. He was to be at a people's rally on the outskirts of Managua at noon. They were to go in, find a setup, take him and anyone else they could hit on the platform out, then bug out during the confusion, relying on their uniforms to get them past the sentries. Then they'd hit the road again and return to the chopper, get on, and get the hell out. Simple, *right!*

Juliano hissed, "The first checkpoint is coming up. Get ready."

Gearing down, Juliano kept his face as serious-looking as he could get it, as though there were nothing in the world more important than driving these foreigners around his country. Most of his countrymen felt the same way. The checkpoint was standard issue: a striped metal pole across the road, a guardhouse, and a sandbagged machine-gun emplacement with the guns pointing both ways on the road.

The sentries were young, the oldest, Delfino Gomez, not more than nineteen. He was hoping to be selected for training in Cuba and possibly Moscow later that year. His heart pounded when he saw the uniforms. He was the exception to the rule, a devout Communist of international thinking. And here, right in front of him, was the perfect example of international communism at work, lending aid: a Sandinista, a Vietnamese, and a Russian colonel. He felt very proud.

Stepping forward to ask for their papers, Gomez's feelings were severely wounded when Juliano attacked him.

"What is that?" He pointed to the machine-gun nest where one of the guns was pointed more or less in their general direction. "Do you have any idea of who I have the honor of escorting? And you, you fool, have your men aiming a machine-gun at them! A machine-gun, I might add, that they were kind enough to give us so we can defend ourselves. Well? Well? What do you have to say for yourself? And where is your salute? These men are entitled to full military courtesy. Show them at least that!"

Gomez nearly lost control of his water. Trying to salute and find the right words at the same time, he failed miserably at both.

Juliano snapped at him in indignation. "Well, are you going to keep us waiting out here in the sun all day? Get on with it, you idiot. We have an appointment with Colonel Rasnovitch."

Delfino Gomez nearly fainted. It was through Rasnovitch's hands that his request for training in Cuba and Moscow was being processed. All he wanted was to be rid of this embarrassment before it ended a promising career.

He yelled to the sentries, "Open up, hurry, these are important men with much to do."

The striped pole rose. Juliano drove through, not looking right or left, ignoring the awkward salutes rendered them by the terrified sentries.

Rossen's back was a cold, sweaty clot. Tomanaga looked as though he did that kind of crap every day. Not the least bit concerned.

Juliano sighed. "Okay, we're through now. Let's get onto the plaza. It's only about three kilometers from here, and there is a hill to the east of the plaza where you can set up. From the crest of the hill to the stands should be between five hundred and six hundred meters."

His riders didn't respond. They heard him, but they had their minds on other things: Tomanaga's was on ice cream and Rossen's on Freddie's, where there was cold beer and quiet company.

Guzman hung up the black telephone, his hands and armpits breaking out in spontaneous sweat. An informant had told one of his agents that professional assassins were indeed coming after him. He was to be killed.

They were in the country even now, coming for him. He had called Rasnovitch to request assistance and advice. It had done no good; he would have to handle things himself. He could not miss the day's meeting; Rasnovitch was to be there, and if the Russian wasn't afraid to go, then he had to go as well.

He could, however, increase security. Looking at his watch, he realized he was late already. He had to go. But first . . . He told his secretary to have two full companies called out of their barracks and put to making a sweep of the plaza. They were to watch for a big gringo and an Oriental. That combination should not be too difficult to find, especially as the Oriental had a steel hook instead of a right hand. Now, he could go. Guzman ran, still sweating.

They were in place after passing one more checkpoint. They had reached the hill, not much as hills went, but it would help a bit. In the distance they could see Lake Managua, and beyond it the Pacific Ocean, stretching out to infinity. They set up under the cover of a grove of banana palms. Through the ART Rossen read the distance. Juliano was right. The stands were decorated with pictures of Sandino in his cowboy hat, and red flags for their guests. The range was right: five hundred and sixty meters. There was about a six-degree angle in their favor; they were effectively shooting downhill. Not so bad. They'd had worse to work with.

Tomanaga finished setting up his rifle and adjusting the bipods. "Well, I guess now we just kill time till the target shows."

Rossen nodded. He still felt uneasy. If anyone

came up to the hill, there was no way—not even the
uniforms—to convince them that some kind of bad
shit was not going down. They'd be yesterday's news.
The plaza was nearly full. Looking at his watch,
Rossen saw that it was almost noon. Guzman would
be there any second.

"Tommy, we'll let him get on the stage. I don't
see the Russian, but whichever way they're placed,
you take the one on the right and I'll take the left.
Two rounds for each of them, then burn up the stands
with one full magazine. Then we split."

"Okay, Jim, you got it."

Juliano was keeping a watch to their rear when
Tomanaga hissed at them, "Boys, we got company."
Rossen moved to his scope. People were gathering
on the stage. A few Cubans, mostly Castro lookalikes,
but no sign of the Russian or Guzman, though several other official-looking types were there.

"What do you mean, company?"

"To your far left." Moving his scope, Rossen saw
what Tomanaga meant. Truckloads of soldiers were
unloading and spreading out in front of the stands,
another group was at the far side of the plaza, and on
the side nearest them was forming a skirmish line,
coming their way.

"Juliano, we got big trouble. What do we do?"

Juliano took in the situation. "They know we're
here. There's no reason to hide it. Kill whoever you
can on the stands, and let's get out."

Rossen grunted. He knew this was going to be
bad. *Buena suerte, my ass!* he thought. Pulling the
butt plate to his shoulder, he nodded at Tomanaga.
"Okay, let's get to work. Take the right, I'll take the
left, and we'll work to the center. Let's go!"

The M-14s began speaking. With the suppressors, it was hard for those below to tell just where the shots were coming from. Those the bullets hit couldn't have cared less; they were for the most part dead. Eleven men went down, mostly Cubans. Guzman had come, but he was behind the stage when the first shots struck. Even then one nearly took his face off.

The crowd in the plaza broke into panic. People ran in all directions, creating the confusion Rossen and Tommy had hoped for. Part of the mob interfered with the progress of the skirmish line heading up the hill. It had taken only ten seconds, and the plaza was in bedlam.

"Okay, Juliano, let's get gone." They ran back to the Gaz jeep, climbed in, and Juliano gunned the motor. Running cross-country to avoid roadblocks, they hit the main road only a click from where they had come through the first checkpoint. If they were lucky, the same fool would be on duty.

He was. When he saw the Gaz running toward his striped pole at full speed, he nearly broke his neck getting it open in time and standing at rigid attention as it raced past him. Rossen gave him a snappy salute in return, which made Delfino feel much better until he received the phone call that told him whom he had just let go by. He sat down by the guardhouse and cried. This had not been a good day.

Luckily, the Sandinista communications system was the norm for Central America, all fucked up, or it would have been a lot rougher. By the time choppers and spotter planes had gotten airborne and the first organized troops in vehicles put on the chase, their quarry was already off the main road and back on the jungle track heading for their Loach.

Taking the risk, Juliano put them in the air and raced the small, fast chopper at treetop level to the south, taking the shortest route to Costa Rica and safety. Rossen and Tomanaga kept their eyes peeled for any pursuit. There was none. They had managed to get in and out. They hadn't made their hits, but that wasn't their fault. And, at least, there would be a lot of very nervous Russians and Cubans in the city.

Rossen was convinced of one thing, however. He was damned if he was going to let Topo talk him into anything else. All he wanted was his money.

19

"I think it is time to put our friends to work on the El Salvadoran project. Georges has all the information, and if we do not move soon, it may become much more difficult. He has heard that the guerrillas there are planning on making the region around the mine a strong point. So if we are going to do it, we must begin immediately."

Juliano nodded. "Very well, I'll fly up and get them. I suppose you want me to use one of our planes to take them to the staging area?"

"Of course. This must be kept very quiet. The Russian and his toady already know too much. This they must not be made aware of. Leave immediately. I will meet them at, what did you say, the staging area? Staging area . . . that is a good name. I must make it a practice to learn more military terminology."

Before Juliano could leave, Topo halted him with "Oh! By the way. I thought you'd like to know that as a result of your attempt on Guzman and Rasnovitch, over two thousand periquackos have been drawn back to the Managua area for security. That is really to our advantage; it is two thousand less men they can put into the field.''

Juliano left, thinking uneasily that sometimes Topo was just a bit too smug about some things.

Rossen and Tomanaga were relayed to a landing strip in Costa Rica, to their surprise discovering that it was on the farm of the man they met in the New Yorker, O'Brian. Some trips did have pleasant endings.

Juliano was there waiting for them. O'Brian gave them a hand with their gear, and said, ''I hear good things about you guys. By the way, I saw Virden, and he said to pass a message on to you just in case we ever met again. He says to tell Papa Gringo the little girl's fine and Virden's in love with her. He's thinking about adopting if they can't find her parents. Also he said to tell you and your partner that he doesn't know anything about any gringos going north. The Sandinistas won't admit it, so why should he?''

Tommy smiled, pleased that Virden was on their side. ''You tell him for us that we're just tourists and will be leaving soon. Okay?''

O'Brian nodded his bald head. ''You got it, fellows. Didn't anyone up there in the zone ever tell you that I was one of the transit points for getting supplies up and wounded out?''

Rossen replied flatly, ''No one said anything to us about you at all.''

''Well, I'll be damned. That's probably the only time around here anyone's ever kept his mouth shut.

Well, that's all from me. Juliano looks like he's got a *langosta* in his shorts, so I'll let you go. Good luck, boys.''

O'Brian was right. Juliano was in a hurry, and he got them airborne as fast as he could.

"What are we going back to Honduras for?"

Juliano turned the plane to head a bit farther to the west to avoid a bank of ominous-looking clouds. "I told that you'll be filled in when we get there. Don't worry."

Rossen frowned at Tommy. " 'Don't worry,' he says. Every time someone tells me not to worry, that's the time I get very worried."

"Amigos, all I can tell you right now is, you are going to have an opportunity to make a great deal of money. Enough to perhaps even give you a retirement plan."

Tommy looked out the window. They were staying low after coming back inland. The Contra plane had flown out to sea to avoid Nicaraguan airspace, then back in once they were over El Salvador. Now they should be over Honduras, passing over Choluteca province, then heading a bit to the northwest to Intipucá. "Look at it this way, buddy. We can always turn the deal down if we don't like it."

Rossen wasn't mollified. But there was little choice. They hadn't known where they were going until Juliano had them in the air.

"How much longer till we set down?"

Juliano checked his watch. "About an hour. We'll be putting down on a small strip by Georges's mine. Till then you might as well enjoy the ride."

Yeah, enjoy the ride, Rossen thought, still a bit pissed off. And he was pissed that Tommy seemed to be doing just that.

The air started getting bumpy, preventing Rossen from getting any sleep. When the aircraft began a steep falling bank to starboard, he knew they were making their approach. To the left he could see the open-pit silver mine. Juliano straightened the plane out, and made one pass over a narrow dirt strip. They could see men and a couple of vehicles parked alongside it, waiting.

"That's our reception party. Let's go in."

Juliano set the plane down easy as a feather, then taxied over to a wooden shed and cut off the motors. Once they were out of the plane, two campesinos hauled it into the shed and closed the doors.

Georges rode up to them in his Land Cruiser. "Welcome back, my friends. If you'll get in, Topo is waiting for you, and we have much to talk about."

Their equipment was put in the rear of the Land Cruiser. Juliano climbed in the front seat with Georges, leaving the rear to Tommy and Rossen.

The other vehicle was a Korean War vintage US jeep with two armed men in it in addition to the driver. It went on ahead the half mile to the mine office buildings, going through the barbed wire and stopping at the office.

As Georges had said, Topo was there waiting, all smiles and exuding goodwill and cheer. He greeted them profusely, which did nothing to make Rossen feel any more reassured.

"Cut the crap, Topo. Just tell us in simple, easy words what it is you want us to do. And no bullshit, or we pull out now."

Topo eyed Georges, who nodded his head in agreement.

"Very well. Please, sit down, señores." He led them to a plank table covered with charts. There was a chair ready for each of them. When everyone was settled, he began.

"Georges told you once that he had a mine in El Salvador. It was a good-paying operation; he hit a very rich vein and worked it for two years. Like most of the miners, he had a portable smelting operation, and the gold is in ingots waiting. All in all, he says that he recovered some five hundred and fifty pounds of gold."

Tommy whistled. Five hundred and fifty pounds of gold! "That's something around five or six million dollars worth, isn't it?"

Georges nodded. "Yes, it is."

Topo regained control of the story with Georges's consent. "If you wonder why our friend here is not living it up on the French Riviera, it is because he did not get the gold out. The Communists attacked the mine, hoping to take it for themselves, but they never found it. It is still there, and we are going to go after it. Georges will give us one half for our services and we'll give you men one hundred thousand dollars for your help."

Tommy leaned forward, his eyes steady, unblinking, no sign of emotion. "How long do you figure this will take?"

Juliano pointed to the chart. "If we can do this right, we will be in and out on the same day."

Rossen looked at Tommy and nodded his head toward the door.

"I think me and Rossen ought to talk this over a bit first. Okay?"

"Certainly, my friends. But remember, we need the gold very badly. Since we have been cut off from any direct support from your government, the gold is desperately needed for supplies. Please give it your most serious consideration. We will answer any and all questions. The only clause is that if you should decide not to go, you will have to be isolated until the operation is over. We are going to try for it even if you are not with us."

They left the shack and walked to the edge of the pit, where they leaned against poles holding up strands of barbed wire.

"What do you think, Tommy?"

"It's a lot of money, and they wouldn't want to pay that much unless they expect the shit to get pretty deep for us. I say, let's find out the rest of the plan, then make a final decision. For right now, let's give it a tentative go based on the plan. Okay?"

Rossen thought a moment. "Yeah, I guess so."

Returning to the men inside, Tommy sat back down. "We're with you if we like the plan. But don't think we're stupid. We know there has to be a reason for you to pay us that much money. You've got plenty of troops, so there has to be something else you need us for."

Juliano watched them, his eyes serious, sympathetic.

"You are right, of course. The reason is, simply, that I don't think the odds on our getting out alive are very good. What we want you to do is be our rear guard. The only way to get back out with the gold is by air. To reach the only field where we can set down, we will have to go through a narrow pass. Our men have plenty of spirit, but they do not have the expertise. We want you to hold this pass for us until we get the gold loaded and off the ground. A second flight, probably a helicopter, will come in for you.

"Once we are on the ground, the Communists will react very strongly. They are well organized and have antiaircraft guns and rockets. If they didn't, we would send the helicopter right into the camp. But we can't take a chance on losing the gold. Therefore, we have to carry it out to the landing strip." He paused to pour a drink of water.

"As for the plan, we also wish your advice on that. But first I want you to walk over every square inch of *this* site. Georges built this area so it was nearly identical to that of the mine in El Salvador."

Rossen bobbed his head in agreement. "Good. It will help us, being able to rehearse the job. We want to see the charts of the area and any aerial photos you might have. In fact, we want new ones taken right now to see just what their defenses are."

Topo rose from his chair. "Señores, I have to return. Juliano will stay with you, and I would also like you to know that the men here at the mine are all trained regular army soldiers. They are to be our commando team. From now on they will take any orders you choose to give them." He looked at his watch. "I will return when you send me the signal that we are ready to go in."

Tommy eyed Topo as though he were retarded. "You're going to go in with us?"

"But of course. If I can ask you two to perhaps die for us, then the least I can do is to be there myself and share the risks. Don't be concerned, gentlemen. I have had much training, and Juliano will tell you that

I have spent my time in the jungle paying . . . what do you call it? Paying my dues?"

Topo took off, leaving them in the care of Georges and Juliano, who settled them into one of the huts on the hill. Juliano had some aerial photos taken of the mine within the last month. He was right; as near as they could tell, it did look a lot like the area they were in now.

They spent the day doing "what-ifs" and walking around the mine, looking at the total layout to get a feel of it and of how much time it would take to move from one place to another, trying the job on in their minds.

"Juliano," Rossen said, stopping by a flat-bed truck, "when do we find out just where the gold is? That's important if we're going to be able to figure out how to get in and out before we get our own asses chewed up."

Juliano indicated the buildings on the hill where the mine offices and cookhouse were. "The gold is up there somewhere. I don't know just where, and even Topo doesn't. Only Georges knows for sure, and he won't say. And to tell the truth, I don't blame him. For now it is, according to him, enough if we can take the mine operations area and hold it for ten minutes. If we can give him that, then he says we'll get the gold." From his pocket he took out one of the air shots of the El Salvador mine. "Once we get here, we'll have to move out to the south. The major difference is there's not a mountain sitting behind us. That mountain is what we'll have to exfiltrate through. The Communists keep a patrol in there all the time, but they're looking for an attack to come at them from the outside. We'll take them from the rear."

Tommy sidled over to them. "I've been wanting to ask you about that. How do we get into the mine area to begin with?"

Juliano lit a Delta, inhaled deeply, and let it out slowly. "We jump in."

Nobody said a word. It had been a long time since Rossen or Tommy had been hooked up, and then they'd been going in with men they knew and trusted all the way. Other Americans. The men in Georges's employ might be reliable; then again, they might not be, and to jump into the mine was touchy. If they didn't have things down to a science, the guerrillas would eat their ass up before they hit the ground. From the photos Rossen had seen, there were not only LMG emplacements along the rim of the pit, there were also some heavy machine-guns that could play hell with any kind of troop transport.

"How many of the guards here will we be able to use?"

Juliano butted out his smoke. "All but five who will remain here."

Rossen thought about it for a minute. "Okay, if that's the way it is, that's the way it is. Tommy, I want you and Juliano to take over their training. I want to take another look at all the pictures of the operational area and try to see where we can best set our feet down, providing we're able to set them down and not just streamer in.

"Tommy, I also want you to weed through our troops and find me some good solid types without too much imagination to be trained as the ones to take out the blocking force in the pass.

"Okay, until we get more information, let's just break this thing up into categories of things we know have to be done anyway. When we get some more input, we'll add whatever else is necessary. Got it?''

Juliano thought for a moment about contesting Rossen's right to give orders, then decided against it. The gringo had more experience; what he was saying made sense. It was organized. Saluting Rossen with a flamboyant sweep of his hand, he made a bow. "At your orders, *Comandante*."

Rossen ignored him, though he knew exactly what had taken place in the change of leadership. But if he and Tommy were to put their asses on the line again, he was damned sure going to have something to say about the way it went down. They'd gone back to training shooters after the Managua fiasco, but Juliano talked them into meeting with Topo one more time, saying Topo wanted to make it up to them. Bet your ass he did!

"Okay, Juliano. Let's get to it. We'll meet in the bunkhouse at dark and talk things over. Any ideas or requests for equipment will be looked at then. And we're going to need some things you might not like or understand, and I don't feel like explaining them. But if we're going to do the job, then it has to be that way."

Juliano gave a Latin shrug. "Just tell me what you want and I'll pass it on to Topo. As far as I'm concerned, I'm content to let you run the show."

"Good enough. For right now, I want you to find Sam Benson and contract him. I think we're going to need him."

20

Tomanaga led the way down. Roberto and Negron were like monkeys on the ropes, taking to rappelling as naturally as if they'd been born with tails. They thought it was great fun to skip down the face of the mountain cliff. Looking up, Tomanaga couldn't see the top of the cliff; they had passed through the fog level and their thin lines were hanging like fakirs' ropes dangling from nothingness.

Swiftly, silently, the hiss of the rope passing through gloved hands was the only sound, and that was muted by the thick air of the pre-dawn. They hit the lip of the ridge they wanted and released their umbilical cords, freeing themselves of the lines. Tomanaga passed Roberto and Negron in the dark, going ahead of them a few paces. They waited for what their leader should want or do next.

Tommy removed the Starlight from its case, attaching it to the M-14. Turning on the scope, he scanned the area. Taking his time, he went over every yard of ground and canyon wall that could be brought into view.

It was time again, time to become not a person but part of another existence, another place, where the mind was only a casual observer detached from the things that were to come or had happened in the past. He breathed deeply, holding the air in, compressing it to the bottom of his lungs, and then releasing only a third of it. He repeated the process again and again, until the new breathing pattern was natural. His senses calmed. Tremors from the night's strain, which had settled in his muscles and tendons, flowed out; he had a "Mind Like Moon," clear, sharp.

Roberto and Negron sensed that Tomanaga was going through some ancient ritual; their Indian blood told them that. They waited, respecting his need.

They didn't have to be told that there was to be no more talking. Not a word would be spoken until the killing began. It was time to go hunting and to hunt silently. They crept along the ledge, keeping always to the deeper shadows, moving slowly, steadily, one step, then another, Tomanaga leading, his mind feeling the way. He listened to his body, letting it guide him along the narrow ridge. Each time they made a turn, or a new vista came into view, they stopped, and Tommy put the scope to his eye and watched. The green haze of the light-gathering device was comforting; it gave one a feeling of power to see where others could not, to look out on a world that couldn't see you. It was almost the gift of invisibility.

He moved on. Not too much farther below them he could make out the trail that Roberto and his party would have to take—dark, silent, but alive. Animals

lived and died in the dark of the pass. Soon men
would die.

Pulling back the flap on his watch, Tommy checked
the time. They were on schedule. It was going well
and there was no need to rush or to make haste that
could cause mistakes.

One more turn around a narrow ledge. They had to
use the tips of their boots to keep from falling. Face
to the wall, bodies pressed against the clammy stone,
they made the turn. Tomanaga raised his hand, then
lowered it to the earth. They hunched over. Tomanaga
moved forward a few paces ahead of them to a point
where the ledge widened out and two men could
stand abreast with ease.

Tommy halted behind a moss-covered boulder about
two feet high that blocked the path. Squatting down
behind it, he once more scoped out the area, beginning at his right and moving in slow, calculated
degrees until he saw what he wanted: the guerrilla
outpost. He knew where they were before he ever put
the scope to his eye, but he saved them for last. One
hundred and thirty meters distant and fifty below. He
was above them; the protection they normally received from the ring of boulders surrounding their
position gave them very little protection from Tomanaga and his men. He changed his breathing back to
normal. The damp night air was heavy, so heavy it
almost had a life of its own. The air moved and
lifted, rose and fell.

Through the magic of the Starlight he saw them.
Six men. Two watching the pass, the others rolled up
in blankets, their bodies partially obscured by boulders. Two were sleeping with their backs against the
rocks. Weapons lay scattered about. A small fire,

hidden from direct view by the rocks, gave enough glow to make the Starlight image nearly as bright as day.

They had made it. Now it was time to wait again. Six men to kill—and it had to be done fast and on time. If shots were heard too soon, it could blow the whole deal and alert the guerrillas at the mine. They would wait.

Leaving the scope, he motioned for Roberto and Negron to move forward. He let each of them take his time and look through the Starlight to familiarize themselves with the targets. Odd! He never thought of them as men until after they were dead. Until then they were just . . . targets. Not real things with flesh and blood, no wives or children, dreams or passions. Just targets.

Waiting, Tomanaga never took his eyes from the outpost, but his mind traveled, traveled over years and distance, gathering in old thoughts, reliving events, tasting them, then going on to new ones.

He was a Nisei, a Japanese-American born in Honolulu. His father and mother had come from Japan and brought with them the old way of their homeland. Those were the traditions he had been brought up with. They were good things to hold to when one was alone, like now. He found comfort in an age long gone, never to come again. Perhaps that was what made him what he was. Always, he had been different from those around him. Like Rossen, he was a loner, but sometimes in his heart of hearts he would dream the old dreams of the vanished samurai, and of honor. It wasn't practical by today's standards, but had he been a practical man, he wouldn't be sitting on the rocky ledge of a pass in El Salvador, waiting for his watch to tell him when to kill six men he had never met. Not practical, yet there was an honor to what he was doing. Rossen wouldn't believe it, but he was a romantic, and with Rossen he had found a way in which to become the gray shade of a warrior the world no longer had any use for except in museums.

Dew collected on his face and on the barrel of his rifle, gathering in small crystal droplets till they gained enough mass, then, obeying the immutable laws of gravity, they rolled ever so slowly down the slick black metal. He covered the scope to keep the lens from fogging.

He checked his watch again; fifteen minutes left. Raising his hand, he made the five-finger sign three times for Roberto and Negron. He liked the two Indians; they were dignified men who had their own honor. Different but the same. A shiver ran down his spine to his left leg, the skin prickling up in thousands of tiny chill bumps. It felt almost delicious.

When this was over, where would they go next, if there was a next? They: That was how he thought of Rossen and himself. *They*. He'd been too long a part of the big man. With pride Tommy believed that he had given the Phü Nhäm something he had never had before—a friend, someone who would never let him down. Before, Rossen had always been alone, even in his heart. It had taken a long time to reach him, and then he had only managed to touch a small part of him and bring it out to where he could at least live among other people.

Life? What was life? There were so many thoughts on the subject expounded on by men wise and stupid since the beginning of time. As for himself, he believed that each man must find his own reason for living, his own reason for dying. He knew he was ready to die. It was not the fear of death that bothered him so much as the manner; that he did not fail himself when the moment came. Or fail his partner. There were times when he knew that if Rossen fell first, he could never leave him. They had been through too much for him to wish to continue without him. When Rossen died—as he would, if not here then some other place like it—then he, too, would die. An honorable death. A noble death.

He was ready. He was samurai.

It was time. Behind the rock, Tomanaga drew the positions of the outpost guards. Assigning Roberto and Negron one each of the sleeping men as their first targets, he'd take the two on duty. The two sleeping men would be no problem; the dull glow of the guerrillas' small campfire made them easy targets. The other two sleeping men were half concealed by boulders and small patches of brush. They'd be targets when the first shots were fired. They'd move and when they did, they'd die. The two standing watch were away from the fire near the edge of the cliff, one standing near a bipod-mounted light machine-gun, the other turned sideways to him, talking.

Tommy scoped the area once more; it was still clear. The talking guard turned and looked into the dark, straight at Tomanaga. The man's face nearly filled the lens of the scope. They looked into each other's eyes, only one didn't know it.

He lowered the scope and looked at his watch. The time was now. He heard the fluttering of engines far outside the pass. If he hadn't been listening, he would have missed it. They were on their way. Nodding at Roberto and Negron, he placed the rifle back on the top of the boulder. His wrist ached; he pushed the pain away to the back of his mind, where it wouldn't interfere. The leather covering of his glove gave the hook a tensile feel, almost that of flesh. He could feel the give to the trigger. When he took up the squeeze, he didn't use what he didn't have. The pressure was applied through his wrist ever so gradually. His first target, the man by the RPD. The next would be the one who had looked at him. He would take his shots from left to right to follow the natural movement of his body.

Roberto was on the left of the rock, Negron to the right. They were placid, content to be where they were. They had their sights on the blanketed forms of the two men sleeping with their backs to the rocks. Killing a sleeping man meant nothing. They were the enemy; any way you could kill them was good enough. If they were asleep, then so much the better. It increased your chances of staying alive to kill again. Western concepts of so-called fair play had no place in the reality of the act of death. Fair play was a sentiment reserved for those men of high conscience and values who never lived like animals or saw their children and wives killed and mutilated; fair play was a luxury that reality could ill afford. Each had his trigger slack drawn up to the point where all it took was the breath of a child to set loose the death waiting inside the cold oiled chamber. They were content.

The extended snouts of the three sound suppressors were steady. Tomanaga counted off the seconds, placing the reticule where the target would be hit at the junction between the shoulder blades. If he was off an inch or two in either direction, it would make no difference. The man was dead. The gloved hook moved a hundredth of an inch, his breathing steadied, was held. The target's back was broad; Tommy could even make out the camouflage pattern of his jacket. Another hundredth of an inch.

The rifle bucked against his shoulder; even as it did, it was moving to the right. The talking man turned, wonder written on his face. He had heard the muffled report of the sound suppressor. In the green haze of the Starlight his eyes were wide; facially, he resembled Negron quite a bit. Tomanaga let him hold the round on the breastbone, where it would explode the heart inside the chest cavity. The guard's face still had that wondering look of confusion, his dying brain not registering what was happening to him. As his knees buckled under him, no longer able to hold the weight of his body, his lips tried to form the word *Dios*. It was a good time to call for God; he was already being taken to whatever afterlife awaited him.

Roberto and Negron fired less than a pulse beat after Tomanaga, their shots taking their targets. As they'd been instructed, each put two rounds into their targets.

Four men dead. Roused from their sleep by the falling bodies, the two remaining men rose and looked toward the bottom of the canyon, their backs to Tomanaga. Before they could raise their weapons to their shoulders, he fired twice more, each time at the broad target: the center of the back. They went down, one embracing a boulder.

Roberto started to get up and move forward, but was halted by Tomanaga's upraised left hand. *Wait. No time to rush things now. Wait a moment longer*. Carefully, he examined the six bodies through the scope. No movement until the last one. The hand of the man draped over the rock trembled slightly. It *could* have been part of his death rattle, but "could" wasn't good enough. Tomanaga let him hold another round. This time he settled in on the back of the head. The 223-grained boat-tailed bullet took him at the point where the spine connected the neck to the skull. In his scope Tommy saw bone and brain matter erupt from the man's head as if some giant cook's spoon had suddenly reached deep inside and tossed the bloody matter to the skies.

Now Tomanaga spoke. "We can go. But be careful. If you have any doubt, shoot them again. Roberto, you go first; I'll cover you from here. Negron, you wait about halfway between me and the outpost. If Roberto signals it's okay, then you join him and I'll follow."

The Indians said nothing. Moving silently, easily, over the ledge, Roberto went for the outpost. Climbing down, using rocky handholds and vines to support his body, he neared the outpost. Tomanaga never took his scope from the dead men, not until he saw Roberto drop down into the outpost, where he took one quick look around at the casualties. In the green glow of the scope Tomanaga saw him take out his machete and quickly lean over the six bodies. In the St. Elmo's fire glow of the Starlight he could see the long-bladed knife move five times. The last man obviously required no further attention. Roberto was just making certain.

The outpost was secure. Negron looked back at Tomanaga, who waved him on, then followed himself. By the time he reached the site, six dead men had been piled neatly together, where they'd be out of the way. Looking around, Tomanaga did a quick inventory; they had added quite a bit to their armaments. Two RPDs and a half-dozen RPG-7 rocket launchers, along with a case of grenades and, of course, the men's personal weapons: two M-14s and four AKAs.

Roberto looked at the fire. Tomanaga nodded; it was all right to toss on a few more sticks. Somehow, he had developed a chill.

21

From his trousers' side pocket Tommy took his radio, turned it on, and checked his watch. It was time. He knew that just out of sight over the rim of the pass the sun would be ready to creep over the edge of the world. He listened. Nothing. Two more minutes, then he heard it.

"This is Banzai Baby. Do you read me? Over."

His small hand radio crackled; he adjusted the squelch until he could hear clearly. "That's a roger. We got you five by five. Are you in place? Over."

"Ten four. On site. All present. Is it a go? Over."

Benson's voice was tight, even over the flatness of the radio.

"Big Man says it's a go. See you later, little buddy. Out."

Out! Soon they would be going out. For now he had to wait until they were actually in the pass before

he would have any more radio contact. If he didn't
hear from them by 1000 hours, he was to go for the
pickup site alone. He wasn't sure he would do it.

Off his wing tips Benson could see the lights of the
other two aircraft. The sun was just beginning to
show its edge off his starboard wing. "Get ready,
we're just about there." His copilot, who was working as the crew chief, didn't respond; he knew what
had to be done. In the cargo bay the smell of gasoline
was heavy and he fought the urge to smoke.

The other two aircraft peeled off, the twin-engined
Cessna climbing for more altitude, the other C-47
banking to the starboard to give Benson some lead
time. They'd go into an orbit and hang tight until
they were due on target.

Below, the valleys and low spots were filled with
the night's mist, heavy fog that moved and waved.
Sighting on a landmark, two ragged peaked mountains, he began his approach. Dropping lower and
picking up his first checkpoint, he slipped a few
degrees to port and lined up for a straight run down
the longest length of the mine from north to south.
The old workhorse's motors were straining; Benson's
hands were sweating. Just one wrong round hitting
them, and it was all over. God, he wished he hadn't
let himself be talked into this kind of shit.

He adjusted the trim a bit. The morning air was
calm, no off-side wind to adjust for; it was going to
be a straight-on run. He was almost there.

The last ridge of mountains passed under him at
less than a hundred feet. The next depression filled
with fog would be the mine. "Fifteen seconds!" he
yelled out. "Be ready, I'm throttling this antique

back.'' As he did, he lowered his flaps thirty degrees to give him more time over the target. *Over the target*, he thought. *Shit, that means me, too.*

"Okay, Bernie. Open them up and pray." The plane was five hundred meters from the edge of the open pit. Below it was a soft gray cloud nestled in the depression created by years of men laboring with picks and shovels, then carrying the dirt out in forty-pound bags on their backs.

Bernardo did as he was ordered. From the spray valves, hundreds of gallons of gasoline were force-sprayed into the sky, creating a cloud of their own, the droplets making rainbows in the morning sun.

Guzman had not been resettling well. He was no longer used to life in the field. Most activity came to a halt at nightfall, and there was a definite lack of intelligent conversation. He would have almost welcomed the snide remarks of Rasnovitch instead of having to deal with the drivel and dogma constantly coming out of the mouths of the guerrillas in camp at the mine.

Rising from his cot, he left the mine owner's offices to go outside. Nearly six o'clock. It would be light soon, but here in the pit the sun was usually half an hour behind the rest of the world. It took that long or longer to burn off the fogbank that settled in every night when the mountain air cooled.

Through the haze he could barely make out the nearer forms in the shadows, where the guerrillas had made their night beds, sleeping in hammocks or on raised bamboo platforms. He knew the men on the ridge were awake: All those around the upper edge of the pit stayed on alert all night, manning their heavy weapons.

There were no campfires at night. Twice in the past, aircraft had sneaked in and fired heat-seeking missiles from a safe distance. A few men had been killed or wounded, but from then on there were no more night campfires. So far the El Salvadorans had lost two helicopters and one propellor-driven observation plane attempting daylight raids on the mine, but there hadn't been any serious attempts. The mine simply was not worth the cost in blood it would take to push them out. That was the reason that the El Salvadorans left them alone. This was a good location; the terrain made it unsuitable for the El Salvadoran advantage in armor and transport. The passes leading up to the mine were easily defended, and the cost to the El Salvadorans would have been prohibitive.

The same applied to the air. There were occasional minor raids made by fighter bombers, but they stayed so high that their attacks were mostly ineffective, doing little damage. The guerrillas would just take cover in holes and tunnels they had dug, and the heavy machine-guns and rocket launchers on the crest of the ridge kept the less than enthusiastic fighter pilots at a distance.

Standing on the edge of the path that led down to the mine proper, Guzman breathed the cool air. It was refreshing after the heaviness of Managua, but he wanted to go home. Nothing was going to happen here. Rasnovitch was like most Russians, paranoid. In order for the Contras to do anything, they would have to have heavy bombers and equipment, which simply was not available to them. It would take a massive air strike with napalm to do any good here.

Looking up at the fog, he knew it was growing light, but from where he stood it was still deepest night.

From the crest of the pit at the far end he heard a deep chugging that became staccato. Heavy machine-gun fire. The emplacements on the ridge were firing. At what? He couldn't see through the mist. Then he heard it. Airplane engines. From the rest of the emplacements around the ridge, other machine-guns joined in. He still couldn't see. A shadow passed over him. The plane. But what was it doing? It had dropped no bombs or fired any rockets. The shadow passed on and was gone. The gunfire slackened off to nothing.

Guzman stood still, and confused. The mist seemed to grow a bit heavier. It smelled strange but familiar. He rubbed his hand across his face, feeling a slickness. He recognized it! His tongue touching his lips told him what it was.

"Madre de Dios!" He ran back into the shack, not knowing what to do or where to go.

Benson had come over the last ridge, clearing it by less than a hundred feet. He was going in low; the old C-47 wasn't fast enough to do it any other way. If he'd gone in much higher, every gun down there would have been able to get on his ass and stay on. This way he hoped to pass over each emplacement as fast as he could, and be out of sight before they could fix on him. Over the drone of his laboring motors he could hear the pumps in the cargo bay working at full speed.

On the crest of the pit below, he saw bright puffs of light, some reaching up to him. The gooney bird shuddered. Looking out of his window, he saw patches being blown out of his wings. He gave it full throttle. Enough was enough. The run over the mine lasted only thirty-three seconds. During that time they had pumped out two hundred and fifty gallons of gasoline.

He was past the mine. Putting his nose up, he went for altitude, speaking on the radio. "Okay, fellows. I'm getting the fuck out of here. It's all yours. See you at the Largo. I'm going home."

The twin engine began its approach. Unlike Benson, the pilot stayed high, at nearly twelve thousand feet. On its pass over the mine, several metallic objects tumbled out of the plane's door, falling like shining boulders.

Guzman ran out of the back door of the shack, carrying his AKM with him. He didn't know what was going to happen, but he did know he didn't want to be around when it did. He headed to the south, away from the mine. Twice sentries started to halt him, then just looked after his fleeing back wonderingly as he ran toward the south pass. They had heard the plane go over, and the firing, but nothing had happened. Maybe the Nica had just gone loco.

Guzman had made it the length of a football field away from the mine when the first shiny propane gas bottle hit the floor of the mine. The impact detonators set around its case worked just fine. It exploded at the time the second container was twenty feet in the air, and the third nearly a hundred. Propane fumes were instantly ignited, reaching the flash point in a thousandth of a second. The gasoline spray being held in suspended mist by the fog caught fire. From the sky it looked as though the ancient land below had given birth to a new volcano. The propane and gasoline mist boiled up out of the pits in heaving waves of flame.

If it looked like a volcano from the sky, it *was* one on earth. Men who had been awakened by the gunfire stood about in confusion until the first propane tank ignited; then, it was hell. Flash burns turned men into living torches. Eyes melting in their sockets, hair and clothes on fire, they ran screaming—or tried to as the air was sucked out of their lungs by the flames that swam around them. Some, who had not come out of their holes, buried their faces in the earth or between their hands, holding their breath. Whirlpools and cyclones of fire met and mixed, boiling. Men died by the dozens. Many literally had their bodies blown in two when the ammunition on their belts and in their weapons exploded.

Those who had the best chance of survival were on the ridges, and most of them were blinded by the flash. They stumbled for the gun pits, screaming in agony, hands clenching at eyes that would never see again. Several fell over the edge of their positions to land on the rocks below. Mouths open to scream were soundless in the agony of the cyclonic fire. No sound was heard for fifteen seconds, then the fire burned itself out, the last of the gasoline eaten up.

There was no longer any fog in the open-pit mine, only seared bodies and a few survivors, most of whom had gone mad with pain as they tried to beat out the flames that ate at their clothes and melted hair to their scalps.

The second C-47 was coming in and a ten-man squad had already started going out the door before the flames quit burning. They were to take out any survivors on the gun placements on the ridge. The rest would wait and jump to land in the bottom of the mine. Inside, Topo was first man in the stick. They would have only seconds to exit before the survivors on the ridge could get their shit back together and begin to open fire; they had to be on the deck by then.

Roberto and Negron grinned widely at each other. To the north, the sky had turned to day in a second. They had two suns rising. The sounds of the explosion reached them only an instant before the shaking of the earth that came with it. They hadn't known what the plan was, but from the calm expression on Tomanaga's face they knew the quaking earth was of their doing and meant death for the Communists in the mine.

Tommy looked toward the new glow in the sky. He knew that it meant horrible death for many. He'd had his doubts about the plan working, but Chuck had sworn it would go just as planned. He'd forgotten what Chuck had said the explosive effect was of one gallon of gasoline in mist relative to dynamite. Something like one gallon of gas equals the explosive force of twenty pounds of dynamite. If that was the case, then over two thousand pounds of high explosives had gone off almost instantly. The blast effect wouldn't be the worst of it. The fire was the part that would give any who lived through it bad dreams for the rest of their lives.

*   *   *

Guzman looked back, too. If it hadn't been that he knew it was petrol he had tasted, he might have thought the Contras had somewhere found an atom bomb. Now what should he do? Return? The idea didn't appeal to him. He heard other aircraft motors. The enemy was not through. Prudence suggested strongly that he take intelligent steps to assure his well-being. He would not return to the mine. In the pass there was an outpost. He would go there and wait to see what occurred next.

22

Juliano came straight to the mine HQ as soon as the flames died down. He'd seen the first stick go out of the C-47. Now he had to get Rossen and Georges on the ground and get back out. The shacks were gone, blown apart by the explosion, but parts of the foundation were still there.

The chopper didn't touch down; Rossen jumped clear and scanned quickly for any survivors. From the rubble, one man, his uniform charred to his body, rose to his feet on legs that had lost nearly all their strength. Rossen shot him in the belly. Georges came up behind him quickly.

"Get to it, and if you see anyone, kill him. I'm going to cover Topo." Rossen's voice was flat, empty of everything but command.

Georges ran over to where the cook's shack had been. An iron wood-burning stove was all that remained to tell what the building had been used for. He began to throw planks and rubble aside.

Rossen made another quick survey. There was no one on the high ground with him. Moving over to where the trail led down into the pit, he took up cover and began scoping the area.

For the more superstitious among Topo's men, it was a scene out of the *Inferno*. Charred bodies lay scattered everywhere, hands shriveled into crones' claws that scratched at the earth or sky futilely; lips were drawn back in eternal grins, showing large yellow teeth and blackened gums, to smile forever or until the huge South American vultures decided to clean up the area. Others lay facedown, mouths filled with earth where they had tried to breathe dirt instead of fire.

In their hearts was no pity for the survivors. Between them there had been too much blood. The blood of brothers, wives, and children. All who moved were killed quickly, with snap shots, without mercy, as Tomanaga had taught them. No one took time to put the unmoving wounded guerrillas who still breathed out of their misery. Let them suffer. It was good!

Guzman wasn't the only one who had heard or seen the explosion. Three detachments of guerrillas had stared in awe, believing for a moment that it was a volcano erupting. Their officers knew the location of the explosion and an attempt at radio communication and its failure made them move. From the shelters, the guerrillas gathered, arming themselves to head to the aid of their comrades.

Tomanaga's lessons were paying off. The Contras advanced, slaughtering everyone in front of them.

Their only job was to reach Rossen and Georges. From the ridge a few survivors began to lay fire on them. The deep chugging of Degytarov heavy machine-guns echoed in rhythm, and two of the Contras went down. Topo checked each of them. One had a shattered knee, the other was gut shot. There wasn't anything to do except the obvious. Topo made it quick; two brain shots and then moved on, taking out his anger on three blinded guerrillas by cutting them nearly in half with a sustained burst from his AKA.

Rossen saw the greatest threat was coming from the ridge. Settling into position and resting his barrel on the trunk of a blown-down tree, he began to pick his targets. In the expanded picture of the ART he adjusted for range mentally.

Behind him Georges hauled and lifted, moving fallen timbers and boards, until he could at last get to the stove and floorboards under it. With a hand pick he'd brought in his pack he tore at the boards, ripping them up.

A guerrilla rose up from his position on the crest to get a better shot at a group of Contras. A 163-grain bullet took him in the lower jaw, exiting at the crown of the skull. Moving to another target, Rossen let him hold one in the back. No fancy shooting; just keep them down and hit whatever he could.

On the valley floor the Contras were taking more casualties. Rossen was beginning to wonder where the stick was that had made the first jump just as they began to attack on the flanks of the guerrillas' ridge line emplacements. Fire from the guerrillas began to diminish. When the Contras captured an enemy gun on their side of the pit, one man took it over and opened fire on the guerrilla survivors on the west side, holding them down.

So far so good. The first of the Contras reached him. Rossen placed him to watch the flanks and lay fire on the western rim. By twos and threes they made it until Topo led in the last party of three men and threw himself down beside Rossen.

"Has he got to it yet?"

"I don't know. Go ask him. And tell him to get a move on." Sliding back until he could get to his feet, Topo did just that, finally joining Georges at the stove. The Contras continued to lay fire on the remaining guerrillas.

"It's here! We have it!"

Topo rose, an ingot of solid gold held above his head. "We have it!" he repeated for the world to hear.

"Okay!" Rossen took out another survivor. "Then get it loaded and get the hell out of here while we can. We're liable to have company at any time, so get a move on."

From the ridge their first stick had finished mopping up the east side and were scrambling down to join the rest of the Contras. Georges's hands were sweaty, his mouth dry, as he loaded each man with his precious cargo. They had lost six men in the fight, leaving him with some men who were going to have to carry double. The small bars that each of them carried was more than they would make during their entire lifetime's work. Everyone carried a fortune except for Rossen and the two men he designated as his backup. Now it was time to run. Run east to the pass. Run for the sun.

"Get going!" Rossen cried. Gravel spat up in

spurts around his face. Someone had a machine-gun going and knew how to use it.

Topo formed up the column, Georges leading the way, bringing up the rear. They kept the gold between them.

From miles around the mine, guerrillas gathered. Some came from camps along the single dirt road that led to San Salvador, others from the mountains to the north. They didn't have far to go. They had been placed there to protect the mine. The explosion and sudden lack of communications told them what had been done. Someone had taken their gold, the gold they had searched for for two years. *Their* gold.

Luis Guzman kept looking back over his shoulder, his feet heavy, clumsy, as he clambered over rocks obstructing the narrow trail leading through the gorge. *Madre de Dios,* he thought again. What could they have used to do such a thing? Were the Americans attacking them? He had seen a number of parachutes when he had crested a small ridge. He knew the gringos had been conducting military exercises in Honduras with Airborne units, and there was a Special Forces Detachment at Ciudad Trujillo on the mosquito coast. If they had entered the war directly, it could change everything. He must get back to Managua. When he reached the outpost in the gorge, he'd make them give him an escort to one of the other camps and from there he would return to Nicaragua.

Tomanaga bit his fingernail, then self-consciously put his hand down. He didn't like showing signs of nervousness. He would have bitten off all ten if he'd had ten.

Once more he glanced at his watch as he'd done every three or four minutes. "They'll be coming within an hour if things went all right."

Roberto and Negron nodded stoically, never taking their eyes from either end of the pass, where they'd been told to keep watch. Tommy wished fervently for the radio by his side to crackle into life. Not knowing was hell. He wished he'd been with Roberto; that was where he should have been, not stuck out here in the pass, waiting. Waiting.

Luis Guzman stopped looking back, afraid that if he did, something might be catching up to him. His eyes were glued to the trail running through the twists and turns of the pass. One step, then another. He stopped to breathe, and leaned against a boulder, his throat dry, rasping. He was almost there, almost safe. Shading his eyes, he looked up at the right side and began following the ridge until he came to it: the outpost. He was safe.

"*Hola.* Compañeros," he cried. "I am here, don't fire. I need your help."

Tommy sighted on Luis, his finger beginning to take up the trigger slack. Then he eased off. The dummy didn't know that the Contras had taken the outpost, and it might not be wise to give their position away by firing. If the fool wanted to come, then he'd let him.

He signaled Roberto, pointing at Luis, and indicated that he was to wave the man to come on up.

Roberto rose, not showing all of himself, and held

one of the captured AK-47s over his head, then motioned for Luis to come on.

Luis nearly broke down in tears. He scrambled up over boulders and vines, clawing his way up to safety. Roberto and Negron looked questioningly at Tomanaga. Thinking it over, he decided that he owed them one. After all, he'd done most of the shooting earlier. Let them have their fun; they deserved it. He nodded an okay. Roberto and Negron smiled, happy as children who were going to get an early Christmas present.

Luis reached the last barrier between himself and safety. Exhausted, he clawed over the last boulder to fall facefirst on the earth in the safety of the outpost.

He froze. In front of his face, not two inches away, a large blue fly crawled over something. He pulled back a couple of inches to bring it into better focus. A human hand. Fear turned his bowels to cold water, and his arms and hands tingled with terrible anticipation. Tears were already welling up in his eyes when he at last looked into the smiling faces of Negron and Roberto. Luis's tears didn't have time to run down his face before the first hack of the machete entered his flesh at the junction of neck and shoulder. His last clear thought was that he had been right. Rasnovitch had been wrong. He should have stayed in Managua.

Tommy looked away. He had seen plenty of men killed, but he hadn't expected the machete treatment. He'd thought they'd simply cut his throat or strangle him. Luis's head hung on by a bloody thread, which Negron neatly trimmed away.

"You know who this is, compadre?" Negron's voice revealed his pleasure. He held the head up to get a better look at it. "This is Luis Guzman, the head of Intelligence for the Sandinos. I have seen his picture many times. I always thought he was much taller.''

Tommy looked back down the pass after saying flatly to Roberto, ''Tell Negron not to play with the damned thing and to cover up the body before the flies drive us crazy.''

Georges set the pace. They had four kilometers to go. Topo turned as the last of the Contras pulled out. Waving at Rossen, he tried to keep the emotion out of his voice—on the far side of the pit he could see men coming. Guerrillas. ''Do not stay too long, amigo. *Buena suerte*.''

''Will you stop saying that, goddamnit! Every time someone in this fucking part of the world says good luck, I end up in deep shit. Now, get out of here. I have to do what you're paying me for.''

23

Topo disappeared. Rossen felt very alone, even though he had two men with him. He and Tommy had been together for so long, it just didn't feel right. The two men he'd selected had been the first two to make it up to the mine HQ. He gave them their orders. Keep him covered. If he was being fired on, they were to return fire to keep the shooters' heads down until he could tend to them.

They had to hold for twenty minutes, then they'd be able to break contact. That should give Topo and Georges enough lead time to make it to where Tommy and his team had secured the pass. Once there, they should have a clear run out of the gorge to where the C-47 would be waiting for them. Twenty minutes. How many were going to die in that time?

Resigned, he pushed the thoughts away; they'd only interfere with business. Concentrate, let the mind go, the body relax. Don't think, only respond. He knew what had to be done; his body and instincts knew. A face filled the scope, then it was gone, abruptly turned into a grotesque mask. Not taking his eye from the scope, Rossen traversed to the right, another target. Not knowing when, his finger took up the slack, his breathing halted for the space of time it took to release the sear of the M-14; he didn't wait to see the hit. He knew where it had gone. In the chest.

Panng. A round ricocheted off a rock near his right shoulder. His backup men laid down fire. The rounds were coming from the ridge they had just vacated. The guerrillas were getting organized, and there were more of them gathering.

Moving up the side of the pit to the gun position, he saw three men in his scope. They were firing with M-14s, probably brought from Vietnam. *Okay, boys, let's do it.* Forcing the tense muscles between his shoulders to relax, he held his breath and counted mentally. *One. Two. Three.* The rifle bucked against his shoulder at each count; three men died. There wasn't time to congratulate himself, he had more people coming up on the other side and down the center of the pit.

Three times he changed magazines. The barrel of the rifle was smoking, the light film of oil on the steel turning to thin blue vapor.

To his backup he said softly, "Take out anyone you can hit. It doesn't matter if you kill or not, just slow them down. We're here to buy time."

He lowered his scope to below a guerrilla's waist. His target screamed in agony, rolling over and over on the ground, his hands clasped between exploded thighs. A groin shot. That should give them pause for reflection. The thought of losing one's family jewels has a tendency to decrease the next person's enthusiasm. Two more in the same spot. The guerrillas in the pit hit the ground. Those on the ridge gave him more problems. From where he was he couldn't do them the same service. *Ten minutes more.*

The guerrillas on the ridge had stopped firing. *What were they doing?* His answer came as the Contra to his right exploded. An RPG had scored a direct hit. The man simply wasn't there anymore. Another explosion behind them. *Mortars.* That was it: They were bringing up their heavy stuff to pound the dog shit out of them from a safe distance. *Good thinking on their part, bad for us.* Another mortar round, this time thirty meters to the front. *Uh-oh, we're being bracketed, time to move out. I'll have to slow them up in the pass.* To his surviving man he yelled, "*Vámanos, amigo, más andale.*"

The man required no further encouragement. They broke and ran, dodging and twisting. Another RPG rocket hissed by them to explode in a clump of burned-out trees, followed by two more 60mm mortar rounds that had been blindly fired by their crews when they saw Rossen begin to move. The rest of the guerrillas moved forward, more confident now that they had the enemy on the run. Their courage returned.

Those in the pit had a harder time. The bodies of their comrades lay all around them, twisted and mutilated by the flames that brought them down. The cries of the wounded men who had had their balls shot off were the worst.

"Señor Tommy, do you read me? Over."
Tommy felt tension run out of him. He grabbed

the radio. "Yeah, I read you fine. Where are you? How's my buddy?"

Topo was nearly as relieved as Tommy. "We're in the mouth of the pass and should be reaching you in an hour. Your friend was fine when I last saw him, but we have heard mortar fire. so I don't know now. That's all. I'll try and reach him by radio. If he's able to answer, I'll call you again. If not, we'll come on in."

The radio clicked off. To Roberto and Negron, Tommy growled, "You take care of things here. I'm going after Rossen. Topo will be here in an hour." He grabbed one of the captured RPD light machine-guns and filled his pack with fifty-round drums of belt ammo for it.

Negron and Roberto knew what Tommy meant. They had the same feelings for each other. They were compadres. Brothers.

"Vaya con Dios."

Tommy scrambled out over the ledge, slipping and sliding down the floor of the gorge. *I'll go with anyone who can help*. He nearly lost his grip on his rifle when he hit a patch of gravel and slid almost fifty feet before coming to a stop. Once he reached the trail he waved back at the outpost, letting them know he was okay, and headed toward the mine.

Rossen's radio clicked and hissed, but he didn't have time to answer. He and his man had taken up places at the mouth of the gorge under a rocky overhang where they'd have protection against in-coming mortar rounds. The RPG would be a bit more difficult to avoid, but the damned thing had to be where it could see him to do any good, and anyone that could see them he could see.

Waiting, Rossen took a pull from his canteen to cut the dryness of his throat, then leaned back against the wall to change magazines. The temperature was beginning to rise; even in the mountains during the daylight hours it could get hot as hell. Dust motes were rising in the air, riding heat waves. From the direction of the mine he could see large birds flying overhead, slowly circling but not going down. They knew it was not yet time to feed. He took out a soft patch of cloth and wiped the lens of the ART.

"Como se llama?" He thought it would be a good idea to know the name of the man he was with, if for no other reason than to be able to put him on the list of the dead.

"Orlando, Señor Tirador!" Rossen looked at him, most closely the eyes. There was fear there, but not panic. That was good. Fear made your senses sharper. As long as it didn't get out of control, it was good to have a bit of it. Rossen put out his hand. *"Con mucho gusto, amigo."*

Orlando shook his hand. It was a good handshake between two men in a desperate place. They knew each would be able to depend on the other.

Scoping out the way they had come, Rossen could see dust riding in the air. The Communists were just around the bend, where a path of trees with big fat leaves provided shelter from the sun . . . if anyone had time to take shelter.

"They're coming, get ready." He pointed to the far side of the small grove. "Watch there. If you see anything, don't wait for me. Go ahead and shoot."

Orlando emulated Rossen, finding a rock where he

would rest the barrel of his rifle to steady it. He looked over his open sights and waited, trying to control his racing heart and aching chest. He thought his heart was going to break out of its shell, it pounded so hard. But he knew he would not leave this man. They were committed.

The guerrillas had gathered their forces and the leaders were holding a meeting in the grove of the trees. Those that had radios were using them. Now they knew which way the enemy had gone. They called out to their comrades to gather and help them. Those on the mountains were to relay the message until every freedom fighter in the region would gather to pursue and kill the devils who had slaughtered so many of their brothers. If they got through the pass alive, they would still not get away. The message had gone out; they would be met or chased until they were caught, the gold captured, and the dead avenged.

Three separate units had come together in the grove and the senior man took charge of all of them. Major Carlos Cordon was not an amateur; he had been to school in Cuba, he knew tactical organization, and he knew the value of what the Contras were taking away. That much money in his hands could keep his war going on for years.

They had seen only two men break and run from the mine, but he knew there had to be more. They had lost twenty-three men. Twenty-three dead and wounded. But he had the numbers on his side now. Over two hundred fighters. They would go into the pass, catch the Contras, and kill them. Kill them slowly if they could be taken alive. That would be the best. That was the way he wanted it.

He sent out point men. This would be done right. They advanced fifty meters to the front, then came the flankers. He gave them their orders: They were sent out to make contact. Move fast, be rapid, but find them. After the flankers came the main body of men spaced out along the narrow trail.

Their greatest danger now would come from an ambush when they entered the pass. He knew that the men with him knew that and most of them still had very fresh memories of those with no balls screaming in terrible agony until their friends, in mercy, brain-shot them.

The point men came into the open. Rossen hissed for Orlando to hold his fire. They weren't just going to rush in. They were coming in like pros. That changed things a bit. Whispering to Orlando, he said, "Look for the leaders. Anyone dressed different or who moves his arms a lot. Hit them. We want to kill the brains."

Orlando liked that; it made sense. He was pleased and proud to be with the shooter. He waited some more. The point men came to within seventy feet of their hiding places in the rocks, making use of the long dark shadows cast by the high sheer walls of the gorge. But they couldn't wait much longer.

The rest of the guerrillas moved out into the clear. Quickly, Rossen registered on any who looked like commanders. Spotting a couple of them, he knew it was time to take out the point. He hissed at Orlando, who grinned in spite of the sweat running down his face, leaving a clean streak on his dust-covered skin.

Their shots came so close together that they sounded like one. The point men went down. Before they hit the dirt, Rossen was on a man he had seen making gestures with his arms. Three hundred meters, an easy shot. He let him hold one in the stomach, then went to rapid fire. Orlando was doing good work. He'd taken out three more. Cursing in Spanish with each hit, he damned them to hell along with their mothers, fathers, sons, and daughters. This was good.

Return fire began sporadically, then increased until they couldn't even raise their heads—there were just too damned many people out there with guns. An RPG exploded on the face of Rossen's rock. He shot the man who fired it in the right leg, tearing a plug of meat the size of his fist out of the thigh. He was being forced to snap-shoot too fast!

"Time to get out of here, buddy. Let's get hat and get gone." Orlando tried to interpret the words but failed; instead, he just followed the leader. They moved deeper into the gorge until the narrow walls would permit only two or three men at a time to come at them, and no one would be able to get above them without mountain-climbing gear. Then, they once more took places: one on each side at the beginning of a curve in the trail. When they had to move out again, they'd be able to do so and at least have a small chance of not getting their asses shot off.

Cordon was furious. Now he knew how many of the swine were holding him up. Only two men! It was ridiculous! He could not tolerate it.

He pushed his men into the gorge along the trail, the troops in front firing as they went. But the enemy was gone. *"Andale, más rapido."* Hurry!

They did, until the first three men went down. Two dead, one with his kneecap blown off. He hopped up and down on his one good leg, screaming and screaming until Orlando put a bullet in his mouth.

Rossen couldn't miss: The guerrillas were packed too tightly, too close together. He changed magazines again and again, each round taking out a man, sometimes two when the bullets passed through one target and into another. Orlando was in a near fever, his mouth gasping for air. It was almost like having sex, the best sex in the world. He was killing as no man had ever killed before, and he was getting high on it.

Cordon screamed at his men to push forward. They could not let these two *cabrones* stop them.

Rossen was afraid his rifle was going to jam from overheating, but there wasn't any way to cool it off unless they broke contact again.

Rossen ducked down behind his rock, nearly flattening out when a burst of machine-gun fire went over his head. Something was wrong. The shots were coming from behind him.

"Stay down, Rossen, I'll give them some shit. You and the other guy get your asses back here." Tommy was at the edge of the curve, the RPD spitting out lead as fast as the belts could feed through it. In the pass bodies piled up on top of one another. It was impossible for Tommy to miss. Rossen and Orlando scuttled back under the sheltering curtain of death that Tomanaga laid down for them.

"Go ahead and pick out a spot; we'll leap-frog

back.'' There was no time for further visiting. Orlando followed Rossen to the next place they could make a stand and give Tommy cover.

Tommy broke and ran. No one followed. The guerrillas didn't move. Bodies lay on top of one another, the dead and the wounded, blood draining out of gaping holes in chests and stomachs. Carrera now knew what it must have been like on the Russian front or in the Pacific, where human waves were mowed down like ripe grain before a scythe. His men were nearly broken. But he would be their strength, their courage. He would give them what they needed to go on. That was what he had been trained for.

To the terrified guerrillas he cried out: "We will go forward as long as one of us has life in his body. We go forward! They will not escape us. If you refuse, then I will shoot each and every one of you myself and then I will have your families executed for your treason. You will go forward or die!''

His ranting ended abruptly when the top of his head was taken off by a burst from an AKA. His men would not go any farther into the valley of death this day. They'd had enough. Let their comrades on the other side have their taste of it. They were going home. This was not what they had come to fight for or against. The men in the valley were not men. They were demons, bad spirits of death. Their luck was gone. They would fight no more. Singly, then by twos and threes, they began to leave the gorge, dragging the wounded with them, leaving the dead and their weapons behind.

24

Georges and Topo reached the outpost. They had met Tomanaga in the gorge and tried to talk him into not going back, but to no avail. Tommy knew where he belonged. The crackle of rifle and machine-gun fire echoed through the gorge, bouncing off the walls, repeating itself.

Topo looked back as he leaned against the wall, resting the weight of his pack on a boulder. To no one in particular he whispered, "It must be hell back there. How many of the Communists are there and how long can Rossen and two men hold them? If they do live, they will have more than earned their money."

Looking up to where Roberto and Negron watched them from their vantage point, he called out, "Come on down. We have a long way to go and must start now."

Negron looked at Roberto and shook his head.

Roberto yelled back down to the party, "Go ahead, we will wait for the gringos."

Topo could have ordered them down, but Indians were strange people, with their own sense of honor, and for him to order them to do something that went against a basic instinct might have invited a refusal to obey his orders. Someone had once said, "It is better to say nothing than give an order you cannot enforce." He did not want to enforce the order to leave on the two men. He was glad they wanted to stay. It made him feel proud of them.

"Very good. But if they do not come within a half hour, then you must consider them dead and I value you two too much to wish you dead. Come after us in thirty minutes, no more. Is it agreed?"

Negron smiled pleasantly. "It is agreed, Señor Topo. One half hour and we will follow. But first we have a gift for you."

They tossed down a waterproof bag the size of a bowling ball. "A present for the *comandante*."

Opening it, Topo gave the first real grin he'd felt in days. Taking the head by the hair, he showed it to his men. "Look, amigos. Proof that God is with us. It is the pig, Guzman! A gift, *un regalito*, for the *comandante!*"

Making a mock bow to the two Indians on the outpost, he went on. "Thank you very much, señores. This is most welcome. But we must not tarry.

"Georges, take the lead again. We must go." For the rest of his men he took a few seconds. "Compadres, we have done well this day. You have performed in a great and courageous manner. I congratulate you. But do not become overconfident. Behind us there is still fighting, and the *communistas* are after us. Our

gringo amigos and our own brave fighters are trying
to slow them down to give us time to reach safety.
We still have ten kilometers to go. Let us do it. If we
fail, then the sacrifices of our fallen friends will have
been for nothing. Let no man falter, but I do not wish
to leave any more dead behind me. Take care of your
amigos and they will take care of you. Now, form
up, be alert, and move out."

Rapid machine-gun fire crackling in the pass saluted them as they formed up into single file again,
leaving Roberto and Negron to wait. From the amount
of gunfire, no one in the column believed very strongly
that the men fighting the holding action would ever
come out of the pass again. Perhaps even Negron and
Roberto didn't believe they had much of a chance,
but they would wait. It was as Topo had said, a
matter of honor.

Thirst was the greatest curse of war. Their mouths
felt as though they'd been stuffed with the cotton of
fear: sour-tasting, thick-tongued, and dry, gums
sticky-dry.

"Where are they?"

Tomanaga scoped out the bend, then raised to get
a look at the sides of the gorge in case the guerrillas
were trying to flank them. Nothing.

"I don't know. But we can stay here only so long.
We've got to pull out soon."

Rossen washed his mouth with a pull from his
canteen. Orlando did the same. The faces of both had
the same drawn, flushed look. Sweat had forced the
salt out of their pores to collect in white streaks on
their backs and under their arms.

"Okay, I'll go back and take a look," Rossen said.

Tommy stopped him. "No. You stay and cover me. You guys have done the hard work today." Under Rossen's watchful eye he sprinted out into the open, dodging from side to side until he reached the place where he'd first found them. It took less than a minute and he was back, his face pale.

"There's no one out there but the dead. You know, when it was going down, it didn't register, but going back and looking, it's like a picture out of the holocaust. I couldn't count the dead; they were all mixed up lying there." He gave an involuntary shiver. "Let's get gone. I don't like it here."

Orlando and Rossen needed no further encouragement. Tomanaga took point, Orlando the drag. Moving quickly at a half shuffle, they headed for the outpost. Rossen knew that Topo and the main party had gone on ahead by now. They didn't have any choice.

While the surviving troops of Carlos Cordon were not any longer in pursuit, there were others who were. They had gathered like the vultures, hoping to be in on the kill. One detachment was on top of the gorge, walking the ridge line to join with others converging on the far side but still fifteen kilometers away.

It was two dark happy faces that cried greetings to Tomanaga and Rossen. "Are you all right, amigos?"

"Yeah, we're okay, Roberto, just a bit tired. How long ago did Topo and Georges pass?"

"About thirty or forty minutes, no more."

"Okay, you guys come on down and say hello to Orlando. He's a hell of a soldier. You two should get to know him better. Oh, yeah, bring down what extra ammo you have, we're a bit low."

Negron and Roberto did as they were asked, hauling down two RPGs and a sack of fragmentation grenades, a gift left by the outpost's previous tenants.

Distributing the ammo among them, Rossen said, "Negron, you take the point and let's try to catch up if we can. I don't think we're going to like it around here after dark. The neighborhood is definitely going to the dogs."

Benson was waiting to get in the air again. At the strip near Georges's mine he had taken over the controls of the plane that had been used for the parachute drop.

The pilot didn't protest. No one in his right mind wanted to take the chance of being caught on the ground if he could avoid it.

By radio Benson had learned that Juliano had gone in after letting Georges and Rossen off, and dropped a few men as LZ security, along with Chuck, who had gone in with his medical kit. Sometimes it was only a matter of seconds between life and death for a wounded man. He wanted to be where he could be of help immediately, and then had taken off again. Juliano was back now, his Loach refueled, and, like Benson, waiting. They would go in together. Juliano's job was to pick up the gold and get it out; Benson was to bring out the men, returning them to Georges's mine.

It was time. Juliano took off first, the small helicopter lifting easily up and going into a low-hanging bank of clouds. Benson would have to wait fifteen more minutes; that should put them both over the LZ at the same time.

They were beginning to catch up. Topo had slowed down a bit to give some of his wounded a little slack. Just a little, though; they were still on a tight schedule, but he no longer wanted to die this close to success.

Juliano made the LZ. Before going in he had made a sweep, flying out five or six kilometers, then working his way back in. What he saw didn't make him feel very good. It looked as though they were going to have company.

Only one thing to do. The gold had to be taken out before the raiding party reached the LZ. He headed for the gorge, using the route he knew that Topo was supposed to be on, and prayed they hadn't made any changes in direction. He should be able to intercept them. As soon as he changed course, he began calling on the radio, gaining altitude to give himself a better chance of having his signal picked up in the valleys and rough ground that was between Topo and the LZ.

"Jefe, can you read me? Over."

The response was immediate.

"Yes, I read quite clear. How are things going?"

"We have problems. I am going to try and raise Benson, but it looks as though there will be unwelcome guests at the LZ. Be prepared for them. What should I do now?''

Topo didn't need much time to make up his mind. ''We are staying on the route we planned earlier. Ahead of us about half a kilometer is a small clearing. Meet us there and we will load the cargo and you can get it out to safety.

''Did you say Benson was flying the pickup aircraft?''

Juliano confirmed it.

''Good, then we will continue on to the LZ and clear it so we can get out. Do you understand?''

Juliano did. ''As you say, jefe. I will be there in three minutes.''

Juliano stayed in orbit until the raiding party appeared, then he set down in a whirlwind of leaves and dust. As fast as the men could line up, the gold was taken from them and stacked in the chopper, canvas straps securing it. None made any comment; they knew which was the more important. They were expendable.

Handing Juliano the waterproof bag Roberto had given him, Topo said, ''Take care of this, amigo. I have a use for it when we meet again.'' Each hoped desperately they would see the other again.

Now it was a race. They had to take the LZ. Papa Gringo was there with only a few men, but they had less than two kilometers to go. With empty packs they could make it in twenty minutes.

Georges felt lost. His world was flying away, but he knew that no one was going to fly out on the chopper. They would all go on the plane or not at all. Stoically, he accepted his plight and checked the magazine on his rifle.

*   *   *

Topo wiped his arm across his forehead. "Compañeros," he said, "it looks as though we may have one more fight. It is possible the Communists will be at the LZ, so we are in a race. It is double-time for the next two kilometers. Check your weapons and make ready. If anyone falls behind, he will be left." The walking wounded looked at one another, their faces drawn and grim. They had come this far and were determined that they would find the strength to make just two more kilometers.

They pushed forward.

Chuck and the LZ party had cleared off as much debris from the landing strip as possible, moving rocks and limbs out of the way to provide a semi-clear lane for the C-47 to set down on. He had heard the conversation with Topo and knew what was coming down. So did Benson. He also knew that Juliano had stayed away from the LZ to avoid drawing attention to it. Benson had passed over Chuck, then banked to starboard and had gone into an orbit fifteen miles to the east, hoping to draw the guerrillas to that location and away from the real LZ.

It didn't work. The Contras weren't the only ones with radios. The raiding party had been spotted and their route of march reported. The guerrillas were converging on what they knew was the only place on the Contras' route of march where a large plane could set down. They would be at the clearing when the Contras arrived.

Chuck picked a small piece of high ground. Not really *high*, but raised a bit above the rest of the clearing, giving him the best field of fire if the guerrillas came in from any direction but the north. That was where he knew Topo and his party should be approaching from. He didn't have enough men to defend the entire field. One LMG and three men with the usual mixture of American and Russian weapons, a few grenades, and that was it. He hoped that Topo had good legs. It was liable to get hairy.

Rossen hadn't heard any of the transmissions; as far as he knew, everything was in order and he was just pushing to catch up.

He was making good time when he reached the spot where Topo had transferred the gold to the Loach. Reading the signs on the ground, it wasn't hard to figure out what was happening. The transfer to the Loach hadn't been part of the original plan, so something must have changed. The Contras were still heading for the LZ, and from the signs left on the ground by their boots they were less than half an hour ahead. The thin ridge of crust around the edge of the bootprints hadn't fully dried, and the temperature was in the nineties.

He pushed on another click, then he heard something and understood. The chatter of automatic-weapons fire! There was a fight going on at the LZ. The guerrillas had caught up.

"Okay, amigos, we got some more work to do and we're going to have to move fast or it'll be too late. You can hear what's going on up ahead. If I have it figured right, we're less than ten minutes away, so let's move out, but be careful and keep your eyes open. We don't want to get shot by our own people.

"Tommy, take the point. You other guys get in the middle; I'll bring up drag. And make sure your weapons are loaded with full magazines."

Rossen's orders were obeyed. They headed out, weapons at the ready. They knew that if they were too late, the plane would not come, and if the guerrillas won, the plane could not set down. And it was a long walk to safety. They would rather fight than cross a hundred miles of mountain, swamp, and jungle. They would much rather fight.

25

Chuck had camouflaged their position as well as possible. He and one man were in it; he had placed the other two Contras on the right and left in individual foxholes, where all the positions could have interlocking fire and give one another some support. He'd taken the LMG and kept his medic kit with him. His orders to the Contras were simple: "Wait and keep down. Let me take the first shots with the LMG and you pick off what you can. Topo and the others will be here soon; we won't have to hold for very long." *God, I hope it's not going to be too long.*

The first of the guerrillas made his appearance. They were lucky—the guerrillas were at the far end of the field. One by one they came. From the east another group came on the scene, then one from the west. "Goddamn," he mumbled, hunkering down a bit lower behind his cover. *C'mon, Topo, Rossen, wherever you are.* The three groups of guerrillas met in the center of the strip. From his viewpoint they seemed to be having an argument about what to do next. One kept pointing over to where Benson had gone into his orbit; the others pointed to the north and the gorge. Chuck hoped they'd pick Benson's direction. North would run them straight into him.

Oh, shit. He straightened out a belt of machine-gun ammo and fingered the trigger, resting the stock against his shoulder. *I got no luck that ain't bad.* The guerrillas were coming straight across the field in a wide skirmish line. *There's no way we can keep them from getting around us, but not all of them are going to make it.* He tried to do a count. As near as he could figure, there were between sixty and seventy men out there. Not good at all.

Chuck had to make his decision: He couldn't let them get too close, but he didn't like having them too far away either. *Shit! Split the difference. Two hundred meters and I'll let them have it. All they can do is kill me. Which they're likely to do anyway.* He adjusted the sights on the Russian machine-gun and nodded at his sideman, telling him to keep the belts clear and running. Last thing he wanted was a stoppage from a twisted belt.

They reached his mark. *Fellows, come on if you're coming. This boy's getting mighty lonesome.* He fired, not working the classic ten-round bursts suggested by most army manuals. He didn't care if he burned up the barrel; one way or the other, things would be decided before that could happen.

He had aimed low; knee high, the rounds cut the legs out of the men in the center. He swung to his right, laying fire on them, trying to herd them into the center of the strip and away from the bush, where they would be able to get around to his flanks. His other two men gave what support they could. He

RUN FOR THE SUN

knew they felt just as lonely as he did. His first burst
had taken five or six men, then they'd gone to earth,
returning fire immediately. The boys out there respond pretty quick, he thought laconically. One more
belt went through his LMG before some of the guerrillas started to move off to the right and left, those in
the center staying where they were and laying return
fire on him and his men.

*Oh, sweet Jesus, this is it. They're going to
eat our cake now.* But he couldn't run; he had to
stay.

The guerrillas hit the brush line at the edge of the
strip and disappeared. From the amount of fire coming at them, they knew the men holding the LZ were
outnumbered. From each side they began to move
toward the small bump of earth where Chuck was
dug in.

He began to take fire from both flanks. His man on
the right went down, the top of his head shot off.
Probably a dum-dum, Chuck observed clinically, never
knew what hit him. Just as well. The earth around
him was being torn up by enemy fire; sonic cracks
were angry bees by the dozens popping over and
around his head. *This is the big one.*

The firing increased; he couldn't lift his head without getting it blown off. Then the sounds of men
yelling battle cries forced him to raise it. *Shit, they're
charging,* he thought, *I might as well take one or
two more with me.* Suddenly, the guerrillas came
out of the tree line, but they weren't charging him.
They were pulling back and the yelling was still
coming from the bush.

Topo and his party had reached the LZ. Following
the sound of gunfire, they had gone into their own

skirmish line and met the guerrillas face to face. The superior snap-fire techniques they'd been taught proved their value there in the bush and trees, where the target was usually less than fifty feet away and in and out of sight in an instant. They were making good solid hits.

Chuck rose. Raising his sights a bit, he went for body shots with the LMG. "*All right,*" he yelled out, and waved at Topo, who had just broken out into the open. "Let's give it to them, jefe." He joined his machine-gun with the combined fire of the raider group. The guerrillas pulled back to the far end of the strip and hit the dirt, their return fire becoming more organized and consistent, forcing the Contras back to take a stand, with Chuck as the pivot point.

Topo slid into the hole with him; Chuck let loose a short burst. "Where's Rossen and Tomanaga?"

Topo pointed to the rear. "They're still back there, but I hope they're coming soon."

Chuck turned the gun over to his sideman, telling him to take it easy on the ammo. "What about the gold?"

"It is safe. Juliano took it away in the Loach. Now we have to worry about getting out of here ourselves."

"What about the wounded? Where are they?"

Again Topo pointed to the north. "They are coming, but I don't want you to go out there yet. We need you here right now."

Chuck thought about it. "Okay, but we got some wounded here. I saw a couple of men go down. Have your boys bring them to me and I'll do what I can for them. After all, that's what you hired me for. I might as well earn my money."

Topo peeked over the top of the hole and down the

strip, where bodies lay broken and dead. Men that
Chuck had killed. *Madre de Dios,* he thought, *these
gringos do like to earn their pay.*

He gave the order, and three men were dragged or
carried over to Chuck, who went to work on them
behind his mini-bunker, setting up two IVs and placing battle dressings. One man had a sucking chest
wound. He covered the hole in the man's chest with
a sheet of tinfoil, and bandaged it after inserting an
airway by doing a crico to aid the man's breathing.
Shots of penicillin were given all around to the
wounded. Best to stop infection before it has a chance
to get started!

Topo admired the swift, sure hands of the former
Special Forces medic who did his job quickly and
tried to inflict as little pain as possible on those under
his care. A most strange, violent, yet incredibly gentle man. Topo had seen him many times with his
niños, his children. It was gringos like this that he
wanted in his country when the war was over.

The other two, the shooters, he liked them, but
they were not the same. They would not stay in one
place. They would keep going until they found what
they wanted most. A time and place to die that was
right for them. He wished them well. They were the
unhappy ones. The lost ones. Men who searched for
their souls. The Indians called men like that *Los
Perdidos,* the Lost Ones. Papa Gringo had found his
soul and he would give it to any in need. He would
most likely die a poor but well-loved man.

Papa Gringo. He started to call Chuck by the
children's name for the first time, and halted, a bit
embarrassed.

Chuck grinned at him. "It's okay, Topo. I like

that name better than any I ever had before. 'Papa
Gringo' suits me just fine.''

The firing had slacked off, both sides taking an
opportunity to size up the situation.

"Papa Gringo, when this war is over, come back
to us. You will always have a home with people who
are your friends. My house is your house.''

Topo was a bit embarrassed by his own sentiment.
"Now, let us see what we can do about those bastards over there. We cannot wait here forever; there
may be more of them on the way.''

Chuck looked across the field where sparkles of
light shot from tall grass and bush. "Looks to me
like a stalemate, and they have time on their side. If
we can't wait, we'll just have to take them out and
hope we have enough men to do it . . . but it's going
to cost an awful lot of blood.''

Topo agreed. "That is true, but what can we do?
There is no other way. I will give my men a few
minutes to rest; we have come far. Then, we will do
it. But if we fail, amigo, I can think of no one I
would rather be with at the end. It is an honor to
share this moment with you.''

Chuck didn't know how to respond. Latins were
always so emotional, but he felt the same. "Me, too,
jefe.''

Topo contacted his squad leaders by radio. "In
fifteen minutes we assault. Try to work around the
trees and get behind them. I will give the signal when
to start.''

Bueno, it was done. He checked his watch. "I
hope your amigos are all right.''

Chuck grunted sourly. "Jefe, those two could live
through an A-bomb blast. If anyone comes out of

this, it'll be them. Let's just worry about ourselves right now.'' It was easier to say than to do. Chuck did worry about them.

Benson was worried about everyone, and there was nothing he could do but wait. During their break Topo had contacted him and gave him the skinny on what was coming down. He'd wait until it was settled one way or the other.

Topo and most of the Contras made their peace with God. It was nearly time. Reluctantly, he picked up his radio and clicked it. ''Compañeros. It is time. Move out.'' The Contras started forward slowly at first. Topo shook Chuck's hand. ''I will go with the men; you stay here and give cover. Besides, I am sure that even if we do win many will need your help when it is over. *Vaya con Dios, compadre.*''

Chuck felt his throat tighten up. ''Yeah, you go with God, too, jefe, but not too soon, hear?'' Topo smiled and slid out of the hole, moving toward the bush to join his men.

Chuck fed in a fresh belt of ammo and worked the action, chambering a round. Firing was beginning to pick up in intensity, dull thuds coming from grenades being tossed by both sides. It was going to be as he had said, very, very bloody. He began to fire short, controlled, accurate bursts, designed more to keep the enemy down than anything else.

He saw several of the guerrillas stand up suddenly, then go down at the far end of the field, and he knew that he hadn't hit them. Two more broke from their cover and came out onto the field, but they came out with their backs to him. What was happening? Had they gone loco? Then he knew. The men were being dropped.

A figure came into view, then quickly disappeared back into the brush. He knew who it was: Rossen had made it to the LZ and had come around from the back. Another, smaller shape followed after the tall one. Tomanaga was there, too. That would make it interesting. Chuck moved his fire to the sides to keep from hitting them by accident. He yelled over the rapid chatter of his machine-gun, ''Get them, you murdering bastards, give him hell, kill all of them, you sweet, miserable cocksuckers. Kill them all!''

Rossen's party had come up behind the guerrillas. Between him and Tomanaga they had them in easy sights. They waited until the firing started to cover the sounds of their own weapons, and had taken out nearly a dozen before the guerrillas caught on that something was not right.

There is a special fear in men's minds about being attacked from the rear that is all out of proportion to reality. The guerrillas didn't know if there were three or four men or a company. Rossen and Tomanaga had taken out most of the officers and noncoms. The average guerrilla didn't want to make decisions. He did what was most natural and tried to save his life. Without the officers to tell them what to do, they began to break and run, and as they did, more did the same. Fear is infectious; once it starts, it is hard to stop. The guerrillas broke, no longer interested in fighting; all they wanted to do was escape. Not many did. When panic sets in, men don't function properly. Most of them ran straight into Topo's men, who snap-shot their asses into hell.

The strip was cleared for landing. Benson, given

the word by Topo, let out a cowboy yelp over the radio. "On my way. I'll be there in ten. Have your shit together and we'll go home."

A smoke grenade marked the wind for him as Benson came in, the tough old bird hitting with a bounce, then shuddering to a stop with barely fifty feet left on the strip. He whipped the plane around to face back the way he'd come. Rossen joined Topo and the rest of the Contras. Tomanaga was helping Chuck with the wounded, and Roberto and Negron were helping one of their own wounded. Orlando had taken a round through the right arm, breaking it. Rossen opened the door to the gooney bird before it was fully stopped, and pulled out the ladder.

"All right, let's get with it. It's time to go home." Topo translated into Spanish, and all gave a relieved cheer as they piled into the old plane, taking places on the canvas seats. Suddenly, they were very, very tired; their legs and arms felt like lead. The wounded were laid in the aisle between the two rows of seats. Rossen moved up to sit with Benson, and Tomanaga kept watch out the open door. He wouldn't close it until they started their takeoff.

Benson took a breath, sizing up the runway. He was just getting ready, when a Loach went past them, heading north. It was Juliano. Over the radio Juliano greeted them. "Get going, amigos, I am going to be your fighter escort. We came in together, and we will leave together. But first, I have a job."

He disappeared to the north, and then Rossen saw white puffs of smoke. Juliano had fired off a full bracket of rockets. The guerrillas who had been trailing them from the gorge joined their comrades. Not in victory, but in death.

Benson gritted his teeth. "Hold on, shooter."

He pushed the throttle forward slowly, steadily building up rpm's, keeping his feet forced down on the brakes. The old bird began to tremble and shake, vibrating from one end to the other, wanting to be set free. The tachometers hit and wavered at 2500 rpm's . . . he couldn't get any more out of them.

"Here we go!" He released the brakes. The plane began to move forward, shuddering and trembling. Benson kept the yoke pushed all the way forward, his arms straining as he held it fixed, trying to split his eye and watch the end of the strip and air-speed indicator at the same time. The plane felt as though it wanted to rise; air rushing under and over the wings gave it life. At one hundred and ten miles per hour he eased off the yoke, letting the laws of physics do their job, and prayed. The plane hit a bump, then another one, then it was rising slowly, ever so slowly. He pulled back when the air speed hit a hundred and thirty, and the old bird was free of the earth and truly flying.

"We got it made, buddy!" Rossen just sat, drained. Was it really all over? The plane leveled off at five thousand feet. Looking out the copilot's window, Rossen saw Juliano in his tiny Loach pacing them, giving them the thumbs-up sign.

Juliano was pleased with himself. He had returned to the mine with the gold, put it under guard, and taken out the other chopper after loading it with rockets. He had not wanted to miss the end of the story.

Topo came up, leaned over, and patted Rossen on the shoulder.

"Well done, amigo. Well done. Now we go home."

*   *   *

ARDE HEADQUARTERS

Topo sat with Juliano in his office.

"You know, my friend, it has been most interesting, and I have learned much these last weeks, and so has the *comandante*."

Juliano poured a drink from a bottle of scotch. "What did you learn?"

Topo rose to look out the window at the rooftops of San José, and wondered how long it would be before he would be able to gaze once more over the rooftops of his own city of Managua. "I have learned that it is possible to be devious and still have honor. Of course, that applies only when you are correct."

An uneasy feeling crept up Juliano's spine. "What does that mean?" He sipped his scotch apprehensively.

"You know it was I who let the word of the attempted assassination of the dogs Guzman and Rasnovitch leak, don't you?"

Juliano leaned back in his chair. "I had a suspicion, but I couldn't figure out why you would do such a thing."

Topo was extremely satisfied with himself as he explained. "At first, I had every intention of killing those two pieces of filth. But then I read of the exploits of a German commando named Skorzeny. During World War Two, in the Battle of the Bulge, this man led a special detachment of English-speaking Germans behind American lines. He let it be known that his prime mission was to kill the supreme allied commander, General Eisenhower. He never really intended to do it. But just the threat made the Allies pull back thousands of troops from the front lines to protect the headquarters area. A rumor was as valuable as three divisions.

"That is what I did. It was not without some trepidation that I sent you into Managua. I would not have liked to have lost you, or, for that matter, the gringos. There is a certain, if simplistic, charm to them, you know? But it did serve its purposes. When we were being hard pressed, the Sandinistas pulled men back and put them to useless tasks. That gave our forces a breathing spell. And I would like you to know that it is not over yet.

"Through the services of our own delightful Rosalia, I have managed to keep the threat alive. You did not know that her cousin was the secretary for Luis Guzman, did you? She came in very handy when we wished the enemy to know something. Also, her cousin did perform one last service for us in Managua. It should keep the Russian from sleeping very well for a long time to come.

"By the way, she is now in San José. You know, it could prove to be most entertaining, having these two female piranhas together. For not only do they have the same first name, they have, if my intelligence is correct, the same appetites.

"Now, say you understand what I did and why, and then let us drink to our 'shooters,' wherever they may be."

Juliano raised his glass, feeling like Caesar saluting doomed gladiators.

MANAGUA

Sergei Rasnovitch cursed the day he had come to this foul land of swamps and fevers, endless heat and mosquitoes. Afghanistan was suddenly very appealing. He had no sooner received the report of the Contra raid on the mine in El Salvador and returned to his office than he found on his desk a most attractively wrapped and beribboned package. On it was a note from the deceased Guzman's divine secretary, Rosalia, saying that this was her gift to him and how she hoped she'd be able to add to it in the next few days, for that was what she and her friends had planned.

The note was a bit cryptic. With trembling fingers he opened the box. Lifting the top, his heart nearly stopped. Inside, faceup and grinning, was the severed head of Luis Guzman swimming in a jar of rum. Sergie Rasnovitch wondered if the entire raid had not been just for the purpose of killing Guzman. If that was so, then the Contras would stop at nothing to get at him, for he was a much greater prize.

Keeping his voice as calm as possible, he called Guzman's successor and demanded an additional thousand men be placed on alert status and in the streets of Managua to watch for the two insane American killers. He longed for the quiet snowy peaks of Afghanistan.

SAN JOSÉ, COSTA RICA

The two Rosalias sat between Rossen and Tomanaga, their eyes hot and intense upon their prey. Rosalia from Guzman's office stroked Tommy's steel hook, while her cousin whispered in the ear of Rossen.

Tomanaga watched his friend's face go pale.

Later when they had regained part of their strength and were able to speak, Rossen told him what she had said.

"No one knows how to give head like a Nica woman."

BESTSELLING BOOKS FROM TOR

MORE BESTSELLERS FROM TOR

GRAHAM MASTERTON

☐	52195-1	CONDOR		$3.50
	52196-X		Canada	$3.95
☐	52191-9	IKON		$3.95
	52192-7		Canada	$4.50
☐	52193-5	THE PARIAH		$3.50
	52194-3		Canada	$3.95
☐	52189-7	SOLITAIRE		$3.95
	52190-0		Canada	$4.50
☐	48067-9	THE SPHINX		$2.95
☐	48061-X	TENGU		$3.50
☐	48042-3	THE WELLS OF HELL		$2.95
☐	52199-4	PICTURE OF EVIL		$3.95
	52200-1		Canada	$4.95

Buy them at your local bookstore or use this handy coupon:
Clip and mail this page with your order
_____

TOR BOOKS—Reader Service Dept.
P.O. Box 690, Rockville Centre, N.Y. 11571

Please send me the book(s) I have checked above. I am
enclosing $_____ (please add $1.00 to cover postage
and handling). Send check or money order only—no cash or
C.O.D.'s.

Mr./Mrs./Miss _____
Address _____
City _____ State/Zip _____
Please allow six weeks for delivery. Prices subject to change
without notice.

Ramsey Campbell

☐ 51652-4   DARK COMPANIONS $3.50
   51653-2   Canada $3.95

☐ 51654-0   THE DOLL WHO ATE HIS MOTHER $3.50
   51655-9   Canada $3.95

☐ 51658-3   THE FACE THAT MUST DIE $3.95
   51659-1   Canada $4.95

☐ 51650-8   INCARNATE $3.95
   51651-6   Canada $4.50

☐ 58125-3   THE NAMELESS $3.50
   58126-1   Canada $3.95

Buy them at your local bookstore or use this handy coupon:
Clip and mail this page with your order

TOR BOOKS—Reader Service Dept.
P.O. Box 690, Rockville Centre, N.Y. 11571

Please send me the book(s) I have checked above. I am enclosing
$_____ (please add $1.00 to cover postage and handling). Send
check or money order only—no cash or C.O.D.'s.

Mr./Mrs./Miss _____
Address _____
City _____ State/Zip _____
Please allow six weeks for delivery. Prices subject to change without
notice.